A HOMECOMING TO CHERISH

JOSIE RIVIERA

PRAISE AND AWARDS

USA TODAY bestselling author

#25 Amazon Bestseller Religious Romance
#38 Amazon Bestseller Contemporary Religious Fiction

PUBLISHER'S WEEKLY REVIEW

"The lighthearted fifth entry in Riviera's Cherish series follows single mother Nora Lancaster as she takes her teenage daughter on a monthlong trip to her "sleepy little" hometown. Nora returns to help the ailing owner of the restaurant. She waits on Julian Wilson, a businessman. After an evening of flirty banter, Julian convinces Nora to go on a date with him, but Nora remains wary. knowing she'll soon leave town and that Julian's new restaurant could put the inn out of business.

As they continue to see each other, Julian introduces Nora to the Christian faith she'd left behind when she moved out of Cherish as a teenager. When things become more serious between Nora and Julian, she must decide if she will postpone her stay indefinitely. Readers will root for Nora and Julian."

IND'TALE MAGAZINE REVIEW

"A sweet summer love story. Nora is a strong, stubborn woman with a teenage daughter who keeps her on her toes. The friendship between Nora and Julia that begins to blossom is tender and dear ...and the relationship blossoms in a tender way. A Homecoming to Cherish is a delightful story filled with faith and scripture to lift the religious reader up and keep them smiling."

5 STAR READER REVIEWS

"This story from Josie Riviera is delightful. We meet Nora, who is returning home to Cherish to help out at an inn formerly owned by her family, and her teenage daughter, Samantha. Tom, the elderly current owner of the inn, is reluctant to accept aid but finds her assistance invaluable.

Tom is not happy that a large chain wants to put an upscale restaurant in town – one that could draw customers away from his dining room. The chain has sent Julian, who will be managing the new location, to town and he is staying at the inn. There is an instant attraction when Nora and Julian meet in the inn's restaurant where she is filling in as a server. But how can a romance bloom when she plans to be in town for only a few weeks and his stay is also temporary? Is there a way to make a relationship work?

I like the way the daughter plays into this story. She helps round out Nora's character but also has a very distinct personality of her own. Many readers will recognize the way she goes through boyfriends and how she is discovering her own strengths."- Amazon Reviewer

"The joy of ordinary life in a quaint decent respectable town. With the book's perfect cover, nice humorous introduction, roosters, coffee, and your neighborhood intriguing characters makes this romance a delightful read. Josie Riviera draws the reader into the page turning plot and satisfies the reader with a believable conclusion. Crissy's Chicken 'n Dumpling Recipe included. I enjoy the Cherish series. Each story including book 5 A Homecoming to Cherish is self-contained." - Amazon Reviewer

"I have loved reading each story in this series and the characters are wonderful. I love the faith being openly discussed and how the relationships and romance evolved in each story. Highly recommend these books. Each one gets five stars and each story in this series is a treasure." - Amazon Reviewer

This book is dedicated to all my wonderful readers who have supported me every inch of the way.

THANK YOU!

INTRODUCTION

To keep up on newly released ebooks, paperbacks, Large Print Paperbacks, audiobooks, as well as exclusive sales, sign up for Josie's Newsletter today.

As a thank you, I'll send you a Free PDF … The Beauty Of …

Josie's Newsletter

Did you know that according to a Yale University study, people who read books live longer?

CHAPTER 1

"You expect us to live here, in this stuffy little town with one traffic light?" Samantha, Nora Lancaster's fifteen-year-old daughter, stood on the steps of the Cherish Hills Inn, arms crossed, wearing her infamous, *I'm bored*, pout. The hot-pink beanie that she wore no matter the weather, sat askew on her head, a whimsical contrast to her black curly hair.

"Why? What's wrong with Cherish?" With an encouraging smile, Nora surveyed the inn. "Wow. The exterior is still painted white."

"Actually, the paint is peeling, Mom, though I wasn't talking about the inn. I was referring to the town."

"We're only here for a month," Nora replied.

"An entire month without seeing my boyfriend! Four whole weeks."

"What's his name again? Eric?"

"Edison."

"I can't keep track. Your boyfriends change regularly."

"Edison is awesome."

"Edison. Like the lightbulb?"

"Yeah, Mom, he's a lightbulb." Samantha breezed past her mother's comment. "He's the cutest boy in the senior class, and his parents are allowing him to drive to Cherish so we can study together. They're buying him a car for his eighteenth birthday."

"Because he invented the lightbulb?"

"Not funny, Mom." Nora had learned to ignore her daughter's eye rolls, though it was still difficult. "I'll turn sixteen soon, and then I'll be able to get my license too."

"Whoa. Backpedal. Study for what? You completed your school term early."

Samantha and a boy alone in a car, plus the idea of Samantha driving set off heart palpitations.

However, Nora had felt the same way when she was only a few years older than Samantha was now. She'd wanted her independence. Once she became a teen, she'd counted the days until she could hightail it out of Cherish. Lifting heavy linens, changing beds in the inn's guestrooms, and fatigue had taken its toll. Along with school, no opportunity remained for fun, extracurricular activities.

She'd appreciated the supportive encouragement from her parents, and the camaraderie with the inn's handful of workers had resulted in friendships. However, at the end of the day, friendship hadn't been enough. Nora had slaved at the inn all those hours ... for what? An inn repeatedly on the brink of bankruptcy?

Luckily, she'd never been a boy-crazy teenager.

Or had she?

Nora's gaze strayed to Samantha's precocious smile, and her heart swelled. Oversized hoop earrings and a silver-studded belt were expressions of Samantha's personality, but didn't take away from her fresh-faced beauty. People remarked that mother and daughter were mirror images, although Samantha was slim, whereas Nora carried twenty extra pounds on her five-foot-eight-inch frame.

"This little town isn't how I remembered." She grinned at her fond childhood memories—skipping in the park, playing hopscotch with friends after school, and eating Dutch chocolate ice cream at the local ice cream parlor.

Truth be told, her younger days had been filled with happiness. This self-contained community of Cherish, which she'd termed claustrophobic once she hit her teens, embraced respectability and decency. What was wrong with that?

However, to sustain the anger toward her parents, Nora had zeroed in on the disagreeable moments. She'd shut the door on the pleasant times and locked her heart, simpler than confronting her weariness and frustration.

"How do you remember the town?" Samantha seemed suddenly talkative.

"Short-sighted." Nora searched for a better answer, though none came.

"Which was what, thirty years ago, Mom?"

"More like fifteen, honey. I'm not that ancient." Nora pinned on a smile, grabbed Samantha's hand, and mounted the expansive porch stairs to the front door of the inn. As expected, Samantha tugged free from her grip.

I could use some help with this young woman, Nora thought. Similar to most teens, Samantha wanted to fit in while asserting her individuality. On a good day, Nora glimpsed her daughter's former sweet self, though she'd quickly close up, perhaps for fear of sharing too much. An image of a giggling, pudgy-cheeked toddler surfaced. Where had her pleasant little girl gone?

"Look at it this way." Nora kept her smile. "You completed the semester early, so now you'll enjoy a longer summer recess."

"Enjoy? Here? I didn't mind getting out of dull, boring school, but living in Cherish for a month isn't a vacation."

"I didn't say it was. I suggested it was an opportunity." Nora turned to take in the picturesque street—the rows of flowering trees, the orange daylilies lining the sidewalk, the cheerful *Good mornings* from folks passing by. Why hadn't she appreciated the joy of ordinary life in this quaint town? Lately, her accounting job in Richmond had carried more and more responsibility and later evenings.

It was wrong, she knew it was wrong, to agree to overtime instead of spending the evenings with her daughter. Even so, Nora was the lone parent who paid the bills.

"An opportunity to work with no salary?" Samantha challenged her.

"Volunteer work is the best kind." Nora turned to her daughter. "Besides, where else would you rather be?"

"Back home in Virginia." A frown from Samantha. "Or sunny Florida, or an exotic island in the Pacific."

"I'll keep it in mind," Nora replied with a teasing laugh.

They both knew that wouldn't happen. Nora was fortunate to have an excellent paying job, a lucrative career. Nevertheless, she still struggled financially.

The door of the inn opened, revealing a skinny, elderly man with stark-white hair. A scowl took over his vein-reddened features.

Nora shouldered her purse and came forward. "Hi. Mr. Canning?"

He shoved up his cheater eyeglasses. "Call me Tom."

Scarcely the greeting Nora had hoped for. Her shoulder muscles tightened as she approached. "Hello, Tom. I'm Nora Lancaster. We spoke several times on the phone." She twisted, revealing her daughter standing behind her. "And this is Samantha."

"Hi." Samantha gave a half-hearted wave.

4

"I figured." Tom rolled up the sleeves of his tan-colored shirt, exposing thin, pointy elbows. "You're the woman who wants to take my inn away from me."

"Hardly," Nora said. "I'm ... I mean *we're* here to help with any work required around the inn until you're fully recovered."

She didn't dare make eye contact with her daughter, assuming Samantha's over-tweezed eyebrows were raised. Lately, the words *help* and *work* weren't in her daughter's vocabulary.

"I'm standing here," Tom was saying. "I am recovered, and I told you not to come."

"And I told you I was coming, regardless. Heart attacks require rest and recuperation, and you spent only three days in the hospital."

"Are you spying on me?"

"On the contrary, I'm concerned."

He scowled. "Nowadays, hospitals don't keep patients any longer than necessary."

"True." Nora regarded his pale features, the stoop of his shoulders. "Nonetheless, you can neither rest nor recuperate if you're operating this place by yourself."

"My employee, Louise, has been with me a decade," Tom replied. "I can't run the inn without her."

"I'm certain she's a hard worker, notwithstanding the fact that your large inn requires more help."

"Are you a doctor?"

"I'm an accountant." Nora shifted. "However, I can visualize every corner of the inn because I worked here nonstop when I was younger. I'm also familiar with the community mindset, and from what I've observed so far, nothing has changed."

"Precisely how the townsfolk like it."

"I remember when my parents wrote to tell me they'd

sold the inn to you. I want to make certain you don't lose it as they did."

The warm June air stilled. Nora chastised herself for speaking her fears aloud.

"Are you saying I'm not capable of running my own inn?" Tom asked. "I bought this place from them, fair and square."

Nora breathed in. She should be patient and tactful. She had had enough conversations with Tom to know he was hard on himself for not being able to do what he used to in his younger days.

"My offer comes with no obligation," she said. "You know, it's okay to accept help from someone who cares."

He raised his milk-white eyebrows at Samantha. "There won't be much for a young person to do."

Samantha grunted her assent.

"She's ambitious," Nora put in. "She's able."

"Right." His tone reflected precisely the opposite. "Decades have passed. Doesn't mean you have a legal claim to the inn now."

"I never suggested that."

He blew out a loud breath. "I was surprised when you contacted me."

"I understand. I've simply kept an eye on it all these years."

"Why?"

"Because it was a part of my every waking hour while I was growing up. Besides ..."

She shifted.

Nope. Not going there. Some subjects were too personal. Guilt rose—brought on by the urgency to fix what she'd come to regret.

He inspected her from head to toe. "I don't remember the likes of you when I bought the place."

6

"I'd left by then." She curled her fingers around the strap of her handbag. "Moved out of town and got married."

"Your parents were nice people."

Were being the operative word.

She swallowed. "They died in a car accident not long after they sold the inn to you."

"I'm sorry."

"Me too."

"Where's your husband?" He peered here and there, as if a husband might miraculously appear.

"We've been divorced for many years." Nora shoved past the troublesome thoughts whenever a conversation alluded to her ex. Samantha didn't seem to care that she'd never known her father. He'd left when she was an infant.

"Uh, huh," Tom said.

Somehow, Nora felt like her lack of a partner was a strike against her.

Please Lord, don't let Tom turn me aside.

Why was a prayer coming to mind? She'd avoided religion for years.

"I … we can pretty much handle any chores and duties." Nora concentrated on Tom. "My accounting background and experience can't hurt either."

"I'll admit your timing is excellent." He closed his mouth, then opened it again. "Mondays are slow, and only a few guests are here."

She patted her daughter's shoulder. "We're ready to assist and can start immediately."

"Tomorrow, eight more guests are arriving." Tom tilted his head to the side. "Three are an advance team from Fresh 'n' Good, a high-end chain that might open a new restaurant in town."

"I've heard of them. One of their restaurants is near us in Virginia."

7

"Probably several." Tom snorted. "One guy from the chain has already arrived."

"You offer dining here too. I saw that on your website, clicked on all the photos."

"I should update the website." Tom scratched his head. "I usually rely on one of the busboys to do it. Teenagers can do these things in a snap."

Nora nodded. "Nowadays, guests expect up-to-date information." She didn't add that the website was outdated.

"My restaurant has been a success up till now," Tom went on. "We're little, though, and Fresh 'n' Good is big." He tugged on the hem of his crewneck sweater. "C'mon inside. Photos are fine, but showing you the inn is better. Besides, I ought to sit down."

"Our luggage is in my car."

"No one will steal it. I figured you were hard-headed and would come anyway, so I asked Louise to prepare rooms for you upstairs."

Nora and Samantha followed him through the carpeted hallway to an expansive parlor, and the fragrant traces of flowers filled the space. A glass vase of crimson roses was set on a cherry wood table, and sunlight gleamed through the front window. Defining the seating area, a cornflower-blue tapestry rug covered a portion of the oak wood floor.

He waited while Nora and Samantha settled on an over-stuffed sofa. With a slight groan, he sagged into the chair across from them. Life-sized ceramic roosters faced each other on the mantel of the stacked rock fireplace.

The interior was a bit dusty and messy, and countless knickknacks added a colonial-flavored clutter to the space. In fact, both the interior and exterior screamed for a thorough cleaning and update. Old-fashioned dark paneling covered two walls, and the plaid patterned wallpaper on the other ones created a folksy flavor that might not appeal to the current market.

Nora folded her hands on her lap. "Will the new restaurant threaten the livelihood of existing local eateries like yours?"

"Maybe. Maybe not. We pride ourselves on our signature desserts, all prepared in house." He hesitated, though not for long. "You mentioned you could begin immediately."

"Immediately?" Samantha, who had been busy scrolling through her cellphone, came to full attention.

Tom stared out the window, away from them. "The doctor advised me not to do anything too physical this month," he mumbled.

"Sound advice." Nora stood. "We'll grab our luggage, freshen up, and start in an hour."

She ignored the gasp from her daughter. Instead, she signaled Samantha to follow her to the car to help carry the luggage.

CHAPTER 2

*A*n hour later, Nora and Samantha had unpacked, showered and changed. Tom had allotted each of them their own bedroom and bathroom, with an adjoining door between. Nora's room, with forest-green walls, an oval braided rug, and a hand-stitched quilt draped over a rocking chair, was pleasant. However, she mentally removed the rooster painting over the bed as well as the farmhouse pillows. She envisioned the heavy draperies replaced with sheer window coverings to allow more natural light, and provide a sleeker, more modern design.

She wasn't here to redecorate; she reminded herself, only to help Tom.

She'd made the offer ahead of time that no money would be exchanged, and she and Samantha would work in payment for rent and food. Now, Tom had accepted the agreement.

When she and Samantha returned to the lobby, Tom introduced them to Louise, a plump, pear-shaped woman. She was in charge of cleaning and kept the inn running behind the scenes.

Lightly, he touched Louise's shoulder. "She's my peach cake."

She reciprocated with a playful punch to his arm. "You're the kindest man in the world."

He smiled, a huge smile earmarked only for Louise, then excused himself to retire to his suite.

"You're both angels and an answer to my prayers." Louise said. She secured a wiry strand of silver hair into her bun while surveying Nora and Samantha. Her demeanor was kind, her hazel eyes thoughtful. She ran her palm along the stairwell's dusty bannister. "Maintaining this place is becoming more and more difficult. It used to be easy, though not so much anymore."

"We're hardly angels," Nora murmured. She'd forgotten so many of the town's residents regarded Christian faith as paramount. Her brain ushered recollections of Sunday services at Memorial Street Church. She wondered if Marge Addyson was still the associate pastor.

Whatever the case, Nora wasn't venturing down the religion road again, save for a quick need-filled prayer now and then. God hadn't been happy with her decision to desert her parents.

She pushed out a breath and focused on what Louise was saying.

"We're in fine shape for the evening, except for some last-minute tidying and wiping down the furniture." Louise's Southern accent was thick as molasses. "We're state-of-the-art and clean with microfiber cloths."

Hardly state-of-the-art, though Nora wasn't about to correct the pleasant woman.

"Tom employs a kitchen staff," Louise continued. "They can use help in the dining room tonight because a server is out sick, and I bet your daughter would be perfect for wait-ressing."

Samantha nearly melted into the elderly woman's encouraging hug, and a whiff of powder and orange blossoms filled Nora's nostrils. Louise was the epitome of the grandmother Samantha had never known, and they seemed to form an instant connection.

"I haven't waitressed in years," Nora replied. "My daughter never has."

"There are only a couple of guests along with one of the restaurant people who arrived earlier today."

"Tom mentioned someone was already here from the team," Nora said, as they followed Louise to the entrance of the dining room.

"His name is Julian Wilson." Louise flicked her gaze to a corner table, and Nora regarded the man.

He wore khaki pants and a dressy button-down shirt. His frame was solid and well-built.

He seemed to realize she was looking, because he turned. He smiled as their gazes met, a smile so genuine it brought heat to her cheeks and a skip to her heartbeat.

Oh my. A pleasing yet bewildering rush stirred her pulse.

He was masculine and utterly in control. She wasn't sure how she knew that. Perhaps because of his well-defined jaw, thick, reddish-brown hair, and handsome features.

"Mr. Wilson is a bigwig," Louise pronounced.

Nora shifted. "An owner?"

"A top manager. He oversees and manages Fresh 'n' Good's new restaurants, which are always successful."

Nora fastened a smile on her face. "I can help with the serving, but let me warn you waitressing isn't my strong suit." She had a tendency toward clumsiness. Nevertheless, surely she could balance a tray and take food orders with only a handful of patrons.

"I'll observe tonight," Samantha put in.

Nora couldn't immediately disagree. "Okay, although be

prepared to roll up your sleeves tomorrow." With a half-hearted nod, she steered Samantha into the dining room. "And remove your beanie."

Nora's sensible tan loafers sank into the plush, silver-gray carpet. Splashes of color on the walls—from dove gray to dusty coral—enhanced the décor.

Tom had built on the restaurant after he'd purchased the inn from her parents. Considering the flickering candles, the mouth-watering aroma of rib roasts from the nearby kitchen, and the polished wooden floors, he'd created a remarkably appealing ambiance. She wondered if he'd used an interior decorator.

Samantha headed to the nearest empty table, slunk into a chair, and shrugged off her hoodie. With her inky-black hair and fair complexion, she was an attractive young woman, although she hid her beauty beneath oversized clothes.

Nora donned a red-checkered apron over her dark slacks and yellow blouse. Encouraged by Louise, she approached Julian's table.

"Good evening." Nora fixed a smile and extracted a notepad and pencil from her apron. "I'm Nora, and I'll be your server. May I start you with a glass of wine?"

He peered up from his menu. "Water is fine, thanks."

Time stopped.

Up close, he was even more attractive. Surely it wasn't legal for a man to be this good-looking. His close-shaven jawline proved even stronger than from a distance. His full lips had tugged into a smile, but it was his startling gray eyes that interrupted her breathing.

His gaze appraised her. "What do you suggest for a main course?"

She paused, giving her nerves a chance to calm and her brain a second to stop racing. "The entire cuisine is delicious and Chef George is agreeable."

She hadn't met the chef, though surely he was … agreeable. She hadn't heard him bark orders or throw pots at the cooks. Was he proficient or was he a chef who couldn't tell the difference between butter and margarine?

Julian blinked. "So he's … agreeable?"

"Oh, I'm certain. What's more, all our desserts are prepared in-house. Plus this dining room—the candles, the subtle gray color—is delightful."

She sounded like a Realtor trying to sell him the dining room.

"So far, everything is charming." He studied her face. "The rooster stoneware, though, is surely from another era."

"They're still in style."

"Roosters?" He grinned. "Maybe, if you're aiming for a family-friendly and more feminine appeal."

"What's wrong with feminine?"

He caught her stare and held it. "Absolutely nothing."

Was he flirting with her? No, he couldn't be. She leaned away, attempting to make herself look smaller. Not easy in her case.

She skirted a glance toward her daughter, who mouthed, "You're embarrassing me."

Nora drew herself up straighter. "In truth, sir, I haven't eaten here yet. Perhaps try the Cherish Inn special?" She'd noted the entrée on the sideboard. "Rib roast simmered in brown gravy, served with garden vegetables."

He perused the menu again. A grin twitched at the corner of his mouth. "Suppose I told you I was a vegetarian?"

"Oh."

Really? A vegetarian? She mentally ran through a list of options. "Then I'd recommend the … garden vegetables."

"I'll take the rib roast special."

"Wait. What? Aren't you a vegetarian?"

"Not tonight." He chuckled. "Actually, not any night."

"Neither am I. I love BLTs."

Her face heated. Now why had she blurted such a thing? He'd probably realize bacon was the reason why she couldn't shed her extra weight.

"Are you doubling as a comedian?" she asked.

"Evidently not a funny one," he said. "I flew into Atlanta early this morning, then boarded a train here. Will pleading travel fatigue dignify my remark?"

"I arrived this afternoon too."

"May I apologize, then?"

"Apology accepted, although you weren't rude." She didn't know how else to respond. "Where were you before Atlanta?"

He gazed toward the ceiling. "Mars."

Her eyes widened and she smiled. She could joke. She could make small talk. "Anywhere a little closer?"

"I rent an apartment in Pennsylvania." He cocked his head. "You?"

"Virginia. I drove here."

"You rent?"

"All I can afford," she replied.

"I'm Julian Wilson."

"Nora Lancaster."

She returned to refill his water glass. When dinner arrived and she'd placed it in front of him, he closed his eyes, clasped his hands together, and whispered a prayer of grace.

She tried to remember when she'd last expressed thanks to God for a meal. It had been a long, long time. Why wasn't her faith as effortless as Julian's apparently was?

Thirty minutes earlier, Nora had been congratulating herself that she'd managed not to spill food on any of the guests, although she had mixed up some orders, including Julian's. And there was the glass of water that had slid off her tray when she half-tripped over the carpet. Water splattered in all directions, barely missing Julian, and she'd fastened her fingers to his table to steady herself.

"No worries," he'd murmured when she knelt on the floor to clean up the mess, saying sorry. He bent to assist her, blotting water and ice with his napkin. "I've spilled food and beverages too numerous to mention. Most haven't been easy clean-ups."

They were nearly nose to nose, and their hands touched. This close, his aftershave, a spicy-woodsy combo, sent a tingling sensation through her. Now why on earth would aftershave have such an effect? Or was it his fingers?

Abruptly, she drew in a breath.

Perhaps it wasn't the aftershave. Perhaps it was the man wearing the aftershave. Hastily, she grabbed several more cloth napkins and kept blotting. Even though they were now crouched several inches apart, that slight brush of his fingers still lingered.

You're his waitress cleaning a spill that could've left him drenched. He didn't invite you to spend a week in Hawaii with him, thus there's no reason to be flustered.

She glanced up.

He didn't attempt to hide his grin. "Did you hear me?"

"Of course." *Of course she hadn't.*

"Want to know what else I've spilled?"

"Sure."

"A full mug of coffee on a porcelain white countertop that is now eternally stained."

"Weren't your countertops sealed when they were installed?"

"I assumed so."

She dropped the sodden napkins on her tray. "Try making a paste. Combine dishwashing liquid with a cup of flour and water. Mix it together, then apply it to the stain and cover it with plastic wrap. Scrape off the paste and rinse with water."

"Thanks." He quirked a rueful eyebrow. "Did the same thing happen to one of your countertops?"

"Yes. The stain was from grape juice."

Brilliant, Nora. This is not the occasion to have a conversation about cleaning methods, while mopping up water on the carpet in a public restaurant—especially with a man you're supposed to be impressing.

She peered at her daughter. She was tipped forward in her chair, fixated on her phone, undoubtedly playing video games and texting. Why had she consented to Samantha's constant requests to have her ears pierced? One earring, okay, but three in each ear?

Well aware that Samantha still managed to keep a critical eye on her, Nora wasn't surprised when Samantha cut her gaze to hers and pressed out a long sigh.

"Your daughter?" Julian extended his hand to assist Nora as they stood. She was a tall woman, but he was taller. She estimated he stood at six foot two. His crisply pressed shirt, open at the throat, emphasized the breadth of his shoulders.

Her heartbeat again picked up speed. She let go of his hand, breathed in, and flattened her apron. "How can you tell?"

Samantha had plucked a slice of bread from the basket Nora had set on her table and began buttering it. She was examining the menu.

"Three reasons." Julian's gray eyes danced with humor. "To begin with, her features are the spitting image of yours. Is your husband with you?"

"I'm not married."

"What's your daughter's name?"

"Samantha."

He nodded. "Nice name."

"And the second reason?" Nora asked.

"You're both beautiful."

"Wow. A pickup line I haven't heard in years."

He didn't miss a beat. "I thought it was ingenious."

Quietly, she laughed. "Another word for smart?"

"Another word for it's the truth."

"That's three words."

He grinned. He was definitely likable. "Plus, your cleaning tip was spoken like a mother with experience."

Though motherly experience might be the death of her.

"Third, you and your daughter have a silent communication."

"You noted our exasperated glares at each other?"

He chuckled. "Is she strong-willed?"

"Let's say she's bordering on persistent when she wants her way."

"She's a blessing," he said. "Her tenaciousness will lead to confidence. Our troubled world needs resilient young leaders."

"In the meantime, the season she's in is challenging." From the corner of her eye, Nora glimpsed Samantha glowering at her, as if warning her mother not to utter another word to this strange man.

But he wasn't a stranger. Nora knew his name, knew where he was from.

He laughed, displaying white teeth and a dimple on his chin. "I didn't mean to stare at you both. I confess it's my pastime."

"What is?"

"Studying people. Their actions and interactions. All folks are fascinating, and I find it essential to gauge people's likes and dislikes when running a restaurant."

"Nothing much exciting goes on here, I assure you."

He brought his measured gaze to hers. "I beg to differ."

She peeked at his left hand, relieved he didn't wear a wedding band.

"I'm not married." Apparently, he read her mind. Or caught her not-so-subtle glance at his hand. "Nor am I a creep who hits on women."

Okay, so he was honest. And good-looking. Thoughts surfaced about spending time with a guy that hadn't surfaced in decades.

"Do you?" she asked with a tease in her voice.

"Do I what?"

"Beg to differ. Are you usually argumentative?"

"No, though I'm known to pursue what I want."

Another pickup line. Was he referring to the new restaurant? Or to her?

No. Nope. Nay.

He was obviously a man who'd honed his charisma. Most likely, numerous females in ... where was he from again? Pennsylvania? ... seized any opportunity to swoon over his charms.

Nora spun to wait on another table.

"Medium rare," Julian called after her.

She shifted back. He was still standing. "Sorry?"

"The roast. I'd prefer the meat cooked medium rare. In addition, I have a choice of two sides."

"You do?"

"They're listed on the menu."

"The roast is served with garden vegetables."

"So you've stated. What are the garden vegetables this evening?"

She tried to read the notes she'd scribbled on her pad, but he was already saying, "I'm assuming zucchini and corn, which are fine."

She jotted down his order. "Sorry."

"Please don't be sorry," he replied. "I'm quite impressed."

"Because I'm botching up a simple menu request?"

"That sounds like an apology, which I won't accept. You're the best waitress I've ever had."

She smiled. "Which is, sir, a fabulous lie."

"Well-intentioned."

"I'll give you that."

He laughed, which made him that much more attractive. His white shirt was in sharp contrast to his tanned features.

She shuffled backward, then hurried to the kitchen to place his order.

Despite their pleasant bantering, Nora maintained her distance for the rest of the evening, save for serving his meal. She added his dinner tab to his room bill.

"Thank you, Mr. Wilson," she said as she attempted to scurry away.

"You can call me Julian, if I may call you Nora. By the way, aren't you going to recite the dessert options?"

"Absolutely." She touched a hand to her forehead. "Would you prefer our—"

"I'm a vegetarian, remember?" He winked. "I'll pass. Black coffee is fine."

She burst out laughing. Only later, when he'd slid back his chair and left, did she realize his joking response made no sense. Desserts, as a rule, didn't have meat in them.

Too bad she hadn't thought quickly enough to counter.

The name of the game in waitressing was concentrating on details. Obviously, being a waitress wasn't her forte, and Tom and Louise were better representatives of Cherish than she could ever be. However, she'd accomplished her first task at the inn since her teens, and an innate sense of satisfaction ran through her—despite having done nothing extraordinary.

She leaned against the wall. If there was anyone she wanted to tell, it was her parents. Perhaps her mother would've smiled and said, "Fine job, Nora." Her father would've glanced up from reviewing their profits and losses and offered a thumbs-up.

If only they were still here.

Nora's chin trembled, her chest ached. Nothing diminished the sorrow, and deep inside, forgiving herself for deserting them seemed continually out of reach. Working at the inn was payback in her own humble way.

The air skirted out of her lungs. Years ago, she had resolved to ground herself in the here and now, with her gaze firmly fixed toward the future. She'd been curious how the inn had evolved in her absence. Yet in the present, all that curiosity circled back to a certain man named Julian.

He was staying here. She might run into him repeatedly.

The idea brought a flutter to her chest.

In under two hours, he'd had quite an influence. Yes, he was undeniably appealing. When he'd gazed at her, he'd made her feel special—like the doe-eyed woman she'd once been.

Was that a good thing or a bad thing? She'd been reckless and foolish in her teens, though she'd loved the feeling of being in love. However, she'd carried hurt for many years and couldn't lift such a heavy burden again. It would only weigh her down.

CHAPTER 3

The next morning, Julian, dressed in jeans and a short-sleeved navy T-shirt embossed with his employer's logo, decided to take a stroll through the town. He was satisfied with his room at the inn, its luxurious bathroom, a sitting area with a soft chair and computer desk, a king-sized bed, and an inviting fireplace.

As he entered the downstairs lobby, he noticed Tom behind his desk and they chatted. During their conversation, Julian learned only a little about the community. Tom did mention that a farmer's market was held in the town square every weekday morning.

Julian's team members of the Fresh 'n' Good chain were scheduled to arrive by midday, and dinner was set for six o'clock, allowing Julian ample time to wander. If the company elected to open a restaurant in Cherish, he was slated to be the person to run it. Therefore, he intended to peruse the place he'd be living in for a few months.

Once he'd breakfasted on thick slices of French toast, bacon, and buttery scrambled eggs, he managed only a sip of coffee, because it was again tasteless and bitter. He'd wanted to inform Nora, the beautiful waitress. He'd hoped she'd serve the morning meal, but he hadn't seen her anywhere.

The night before, he hadn't been able to catch her gaze after his dinner.

He'd flirted with her when she'd served him, something he rarely did. More often than not, women responded to him by flipping back their hair and tittering an encouraging response. In contrast, Nora had challenged him for using a pickup line.

She'd caught his interest, his attraction. Good nature radiated on her lovely features, and she made him feel happy in a way he hardly understood. Once he'd entered his thirties, he'd found he was no longer intrigued by giggling females who were all too available. Every relationship he'd had recently had become history after a few months.

"Six months at tops," he affirmed as he exited the inn. Following Tom's directions, he found a gravel path and a sign directing him to the square.

An ideal South Carolina morning beckoned—the sun radiant and enveloping his arms in warmth. The sky boasted a blazing blue, and graceful flowers bloomed a buttery-yellow.

He paused at Memorial Street Church, noting its central location, its high-arched windows and ornate wooden doors. He typed the hours of the services into his phone. He dodged a boy on a bicycle and followed the sights and sounds to the farmer's market.

Hope quickened his steps. Nora might be there. As a further bonus, if she was buying fresh produce, there would be superb meals in store at the inn.

A half dozen strides brought him to rows and rows of booths, and whiffs of recently picked peaches, fragrant ground spices, and touches of citrus swirled around him.

Somewhere a dog barked, shadowed by the distinguishable yelp of a puppy.

Julian froze. His chest tightened. It wasn't the large dog that stopped him. It was the small dog.

Completely irrational, he reminded himself. The chance of encountering a dog in this people-loving, presumably dog-loving community was high and he should prepare himself.

He dismissed his fear and noticed Nora weaving in and out of the aisles, toting a wicker basket overflowing with juicy peaches and blueberries.

Julian paused, pleased with his good fortune.

She was a natural beauty, tall and shapely, wearing a pair of figure-hugging capris and a flowered blue blouse. God had certainly placed favor on her because she was a classy Rubenesque woman, and Julian couldn't contain his grin.

People, young and elderly, bustled past, their genial banter punctuated by laughter. Everyone seemed to know each other by their first name.

He liked that. He liked the special feeling of community. So far, Cherish appealed to him. At a stand, he purchased a homemade pretzel dipped in melted cinnamon and sugar, and quickly polished it off.

Nora had wandered to a booth teaming with wildflowers. She scooped up a hand-tied bunch of dried lavender and placed it in her basket. Sidelined by a cordial shopkeeper, she bought a slice of thick vanilla cake frosted with strawberry icing.

Watching her relaxed and chatting with the townsfolk was as pleasant for Julian as when she'd waited on him. In both instances, her sweet smile captivated him.

He debated striding up to her when a sturdy, muscular golden retriever followed by a gangly puppy raced through the crowd. Both dogs trailed their leashes, both obviously excited by an escape from their owners. Intent on chasing a squirrel, they dashed past him.

"Tiny Tim! Molly Belle!" A man wearing casual pants, a shirt and a bow tie clapped his hands and sprinted after them. The retriever veered toward an empty aisle, then snatched up a pastry. "Give the cinnamon roll back!"

"Sorry," the man muttered as he bumped past Julian. "That mischievous golden is teaching my innocent Yorkipoo some bad habits."

Julian tried to ignore his rapid heartbeat as his gaze strayed to the small dog. "Are they … partners in crime?" he inquired.

"Unfortunately." Max quickened his pace. "Molly Belle, she's the retriever, will steal any pastry she can reach."

"Watch out!" someone cried out. The dogs had circled and were bounding straight toward Nora.

Juggling the slice of cake and her full basket, Nora tried to dodge the dogs as they dashed past. The retriever sideswiped her. She barely managed to keep from falling, but her cake and basket went flying.

"Nora!" Julian hurried to her. "Nora. Are you all right?"

She whirled to face him. "Yes. I was only startled."

Julian realized how alarmed he'd sounded, and tried for a joking tone. "I'm here to rescue you."

"From what?"

"I was afraid you were hurt."

"I'm fine, and the dogs are harmless."

Harmless? Julian didn't reply.

She smoothed her blouse and then crouched down to pick up the cake and basket.

He bent near, grabbing errant fruit before it rolled out of reach. "We should stop meeting like this," he joked.

"Tidying up messes, you mean?"

"We were made for each other." *Now why had his disloyal tongue blurted out such a romantic declaration?*

"Perhaps if we were opening a cleaning service." Their gazes met, and she grinned. At least *she* appreciated his sense of humor. "By the way, you're not obliged to help me."

"I insist." Quickly, he placed the fruit in the basket, stood and helped her to her feet.

"Thank you."

"You're welcome." He inspected a couple of bruised peaches. "Is this fruit ruined? I hope you weren't intending to serve peach puffs for the specialty dessert this evening."

"What are peach puffs?"

"A puffy peach, I would imagine." He shrugged. "I saw the recipe in a magazine once, and the photo was picture-perfect."

"Heaven forbid I was in charge of the inn's menu. I purchased the fruit for me and my daughter to snack in our room. I'm hoping it will encourage her to eat more than junk food."

"Young people. They'd rather eat potato chips and drink soda."

"Right."

"Like us."

She laughed. "Truer words were never spoken."

Her slightly wild hair tumbled around her shoulders, framing her angelic face and fair complexion. Her flowered blouse reflected the color of her huge blue eyes.

She was a gorgeous woman, especially when she laughed.

He cleared his throat. "Are you staying at a place here?" He wasn't sure he could speak, but apparently he could.

"I am. Temporarily."

"I'll walk you back."

She started toward a vegetable booth and he trailed behind.

"You don't know where I'm staying," she said.

"Guide me." Next, he planned to request her phone number.

She rested the basket on her hip, emphasizing her generous curves. A dab of strawberry frosting was smudged on her cheek. He reached up and gently smoothed it away.

She lifted her dark eyebrows.

"Sorry. You had …" He held up the frosting on his fingers as evidence.

You're staring at her. He dropped his hand.

"My daughter and I are renting rooms at the Cherish Hills Inn," she replied.

"Me too."

"Yes, I know."

He beamed. More good news. They were staying in the same place. His mood grew brighter by the minute.

"Obviously, our walk doesn't put you out of your way," she was saying.

"The inn is only three blocks over."

As if she didn't already know the location of the inn.

"I can find it by myself."

"It's no bother," he said. "I was heading back there myself."

He wasn't. He'd contemplated stopping at the local Big Brothers Big Sisters center. He hoped to sign up for volunteer opportunities if he was going to stay in Cherish for a few months. The program was community based and directed toward low-income families. Julian had never had children of his own and took delight in mentoring them, especially the older kids. Writing donation checks was easy. He was more of a hands-on man.

He kept their pace sedate. "How long are you in town?"

A smile lit her face. "Samantha and I are here for the entire month of June."

"If my bosses decide to open a restaurant here, I'll be in

charge and staying for a few months. I'll probably rent an apartment."

She studied his T-shirt. "Fresh 'n' Good."

"The food you love—prepared fresh." He parroted the chain's motto.

"I've heard that jingle on the radio more times than I can count."

"Advertising is a sizable part of our budget."

"You're not the owner, correct?" she asked.

"I'm a manager."

"Right. Well, I lived in Cherish for eighteen years," she said. "A chain might not fit into the community."

"Why not?"

"Too … large. From what I recall, the city council was never keen on expansion."

"Stifling growth isn't beneficial for any place," he countered. "To survive, a town should welcome industry."

"A quiet environment is preferred by the folks here." Her argument was interrupted by a woman wheeling a baby in a carriage. The woman smiled an acknowledgement as she zipped by.

"The owners are sensitive and adhere to regulations," Julian responded. "A bonus is that the new restaurant will create good-paying jobs."

She deliberated in front of Whitney's Ice Cream Shop, eyeing the listings and the sign touting butter pecan as the flavor of the day.

"Therefore, the chain won't put independent places out of business?" she asked.

"Of course not."

"At least, not on purpose," she murmured in a quiet undertone.

Fresh 'n' Good had shuttered lesser establishments. Julian knew that. Larger, well-capitalized chains were positioned for growth and withstood economic downturns and competition. Little businesses? Not so much. He didn't share his musings, sorry that reality had intruded on their pleasant stroll.

For reasons he couldn't explain, he wanted to gather Nora close and reassure her, though he wouldn't overstep his bounds. They'd only known each other a short while. Instead, he provided a heartening smile. "I'll do my best to ensure no one goes out of business here."

"Promise?"

"I'll try." He guided her across the street. "I don't make the final assessments, I just work out the kinks once the restaurant opens."

They changed direction and drew near the Memorial Street Church.

"This church has been here for fifty years. Still painted white." She smiled. "I remember it well."

"Did you attend? They offer services on Sunday mornings and Wednesday evenings."

"As a child, I went happily and willingly. However, when I reached my teens, I dug in my heels and refused, though my parents were strict and tried to force me. I wanted to hang out with my friends instead."

"On a Sunday morning?"

"More accurately, I preferred to sleep late."

"Evidently your friends weren't churchgoers, either."

"I longed to fit in with the popular girls, and peer pressure is powerful," she replied. "Church wasn't on their list of Sunday morning priorities."

"Did you?"

"Did I what?"

"Fit in?"

She expelled a breath. "No. In truth, never."

"I'm surprised." He studied her exquisite features. "Surely, all the high school guys were jostling for a position to ask you out on a date."

"I was too busy working. I didn't have time for cheer-leading or any fun activities."

"Cinderella, someone should've taken you to the ball."

She smiled and didn't elaborate, and he didn't press for details. Her gaze fixed on a window box brimming with greenery and silver petunias across the way.

"If this is any consolation, we both can agree that dynamics in middle and high school are brutal." His cell-phone vibrated in his pocket and he ignored it. "I was athletic, but hung out with the wrong crowd too."

"I didn't hang out with the wrong crowd. No one was interested in me because I was never available. Thus, my social status was nonexistent."

"Well, I played basketball, the key to popularity. Only difference was I was dirt-poor compared to the other kids."

"Care to tell me about it?"

He grinned. "Only if we can get ice cream."

"We passed Whitney's already. I'm on a—"

"Let's double back." He captured her hand, and she didn't shake him off. His heart skipped a beat. Holding her slim fingers in his felt right.

Once they reached the shop, he turned to Nora with an expectant smile.

"I don't usually indulge and eat ice cream in the morning," she objected. "Besides, I'm dieting."

"Ridiculous. You? Why?" He sighed. *Women and their outlandish ideas about their bodies.* "Nonetheless, I'll try to convince you of the wisdom of the idea because ice cream is nutritious." He led her to an outdoor table beneath a striped canopy.

"Ice cream isn't nutritious," she replied.

"Some may argue ice cream is part of a healthy, well-balanced diet."

"Uh, huh."

"How about this?" He assumed a tone that brooked no more debate. "I'm treating."

"Okay, then." She grinned. "Dutch chocolate is my favorite, except Whitney's seldom used to serve it."

He squinted toward the sign. "Chocolate is listed. What's the difference?"

"Dutch chocolate is more mellow than regular chocolate."

"I'm not seeing Dutch chocolate on the menu." He drew bright-yellow chairs into place around a wrought-iron table. "Is soft-serve regular chocolate okay?"

"Sure, although I shouldn't."

Her smile was a bit self-deprecating.

He opened his mouth to protest, but asked instead, "Cone or cup?"

"Surprise me."

"One scoop or two?"

"One."

While waiting for their orders inside the shop, he stepped to a quiet spot and yanked out his cellphone. He'd received numerous text messages from his teammates: they might get stranded at the Atlanta train station because the trains were running late.

Keep me posted, he texted, then shoved the phone back into his pocket.

He returned to Nora carrying two cones—a scoop of chocolate in one and three scoops of butter pecan in the other. He handed her the chocolate cone and settled across from her.

She took a bite, rolled it around her tongue, and smiled. "The ice cream is delicious and exactly how I remembered.

This entire town is stuck in time. I can't get over how slow the pace is compared to Virginia."

"Where do you live in Virginia?"

"Richmond."

"Richmond has, what, a couple hundred thousand people?"

"Even higher at last count," she said with a breezy smile. "Where are you in Pennsylvania?"

"I live in Scranton, though I don't call it home because I'm on the road so often. I go wherever the job sends me."

"A company man."

He shrugged. "I suppose, although the company has been fair and very generous."

She studied him over her cone. "What's the length of time you stay in a city?"

"Never more than six months," he replied. "I'm used to moving around a lot. My mother never had us stay in one place for long, either."

Now why bring up his mother? Inwardly, he shook his head.

"Why not?" Nora was asking.

"My mother was invariably chased by creditors." There, he'd said it aloud. He well remembered middle-of-the-night exits from dingy apartments, and the familiar embarrassment and shame washed over him.

"I'm sorry," she said. "Getting acclimated to different schools must have been difficult."

"I was taught never to complain, never to display emotion." Avoidance and running was the fabric of his existence. He'd moved around to establish a distance between himself and his mother, his brother. But now? What was he running from now that he never stayed in one place longer than a few months?

He ate in record time, then waited for Nora.

"Do you attend a church in Richmond?" he asked.

"No."

"That's it? Just no?"

She contemplated the rest of her cone, then finished it. "I wrestled with doubts about Christianity during my teen years. I still do. You?"

"As I've alluded, my high school crowd was … shall we say misguided?"

"That's your whole story?"

"Only the beginning." He fixed his gaze on a point beyond her. He'd tried to add status, add alcohol, to ensure his popularity as a teen. Always the new kid in a new school. His efforts had been successful, although the emotional expense had left him exhausted.

"And?" Nora's steady voice roused him from unhappy remembrances, the weight of decisions he was sorry for.

"When I was a senior, the guys on my basketball team drank beer on weekends. I figured I'd join them." Julian examined his palms. "I grappled with my choices, I knew they were wrong, but alcohol became an addiction for me. I also confronted my conscience, or rather, it confronted me."

Nora studied the inked rose and cross tattoo on his upper left arm. A sign of his commitment to God. "Go on," she encouraged.

"Toward the end of the year, a counselor urged my mother to admit me to a treatment program. I resisted at first. In hindsight, the therapy was exceptional, although guess who helped me the most in the end?"

Nora propped her chin on her fists. "Who?"

"God. He gave me hope when I was in a dark place. He comforted me through my challenging hours. On the flip side, my conviction is a constant struggle."

"Regardless, my watery faith doesn't compare with yours. Yours is steadfast." Her voice grew heavy. "My days are filled with busyness, and I'm no saint. I married young and—"

"It doesn't matter to God. Don't look back. Look forward. God loves us for who we are."

She fidgeted with the slim silver band on the index finger of her right hand. He hadn't noticed the ring the previous evening.

"What about Samantha?" He took Nora's restless hands in his. "What are her views regarding religion?"

"She says little. My parents' insistence has reaffirmed my belief that Samantha is her own person who must form her own opinions. If she wants to attend church, she'll tell me."

"Everyone's path is different," he replied. "Guide her to find worth in what is true."

"Which is?"

"All the right stuff. Our creator lives within us. Stay the course and believe. Our God is a faithful God."

He didn't normally speak about his faith so openly. What was it about this woman that brought out his need to connect—both as a friend and spiritually?

"I try to lead a good life and often make mistakes. Samantha isn't an easy child to raise. She's frequently willful." Nora didn't meet his gaze. When she did, he saw defenselessness in her eyes. He wanted to envelope her in his arms and assure her she never needed to bear her worries alone.

He was here for her.

However, he didn't reply, didn't react further.

They were sitting outside an ice cream shop, and their relationship wasn't at the point where he could hold her close and murmur agreeable assurances. He'd said enough.

He ran his thumbs soothingly over her palms. And why did Nora bring out such a protective instinct in him? She was certainly accomplished and capable.

His cellphone vibrated again. In fact, it had been vibrating for the past several minutes.

He sighed. "If you're ready, we should head back."

"All right." She grabbed her basket. "In any event, you gave me a lot to process."

His mouth grew dry. Had he said too much? He'd merely wished to share his religious principles with her. He broke the silence when they reached the gravel path leading to the inn.

"You're fond of Cherish," he said.

"It goes without saying." She lifted her shoulders in a swift shrug. "But then again, I moved away."

"Why? This area is delightful."

"Delightful?" Her lips curved into a crooked smile.

Actually, she was the one who was delightful.

"I took off with my boyfriend when we turned eighteen," she murmured. "We married a short while later and divorced before our first wedding anniversary."

"You and your ex have been apart since …"

"Since Samantha was a baby." Nora replied in a manner more emotional than dismissive. "Colic and late-night feedings weren't his thing."

So Nora was a long-time single, just as he was. Although, in Julian's case, he'd never married.

He debated how best to respond.

"Will you have dinner with me?" He shoved his hands in his pockets. "Not necessarily at the inn—I realize you work there. I assume waitressing is a part-time gig for you."

"Very part-time." Her eyes twinkled. "Couldn't you tell last night?"

"Not in the least." He opted for politeness. "You were speedy and competent."

"Speedy, thanks to the kitchen's efficiency."

"And your agreeable chef?" he teased.

She flashed him a jaunty grin. "Not so agreeable, it turns out."

"May I ask why you're in Cherish if not to work in the restaurant?"

"I have other business at the inn."

"What type of business?"

"Unfinished business."

Okay, that was vague.

He leaned over. His breath whispered against her fragrant hair. She smelled of lilacs and brightness and everything valuable in life. "Again, will you have dinner with me?"

"I can't."

"Because?"

"Because I have a daughter."

"Plenty of single women with children date."

"When Samantha gets older, perhaps." Nora briefly closed her eyes, her silky black lashes sweeping down her cheeks. "At present, she's going through a tough time. I intend to be supportive and available for her."

"Are you a helicopter parent?"

They'd reached the inn and she paused in midstep. "Julian, do you have children?"

"I've never married. And no, no children."

Dark red stained Nora's cheeks. "Then wait to give advice when you can speak from experience."

"I've obviously put my foot in my mouth and you're right. However, I still want to take you out to dinner. If we don't click, we'll say we tried."

"Why wouldn't we click?"

"I've thrown around bad jokes and given parenting advice when I shouldn't."

They ducked under a majestic oak tree and climbed the front steps of the inn, settling on two wide-slatted rocking chairs on the porch. He allowed the charm of this modest town, the mild June breeze, to sweep over him. Chubby squirrels chattered, leaping from branch to branch.

"It's lovely here," he mused, rocking back and forth.

"The town is idyllic." She set the basket beside her and ran her fingers along the peaches. "I never dreamed I'd say those words when I was a belligerent teen, but I'm beginning to think I'm a small-town girl at heart."

"Yet you created a different life in a provincial capital."

"I craved a cosmopolitan existence—the concrete jungle and all that."

"Now?"

"Now I'm unsure."

"Me too," he admitted. "I'm warming up to the idea of settling permanently in a modest, serene community."

"I've been thinking along the same lines."

There was a connection between them, weightless at first, growing ever stronger. His heartbeat increased, and his gaze drifted to the beauty rocking slowly beside him. His enthusiasm for travel and exciting new places was fast losing its allure.

"Are you free on Friday night?" His voice came out louder than he'd expected.

She hesitated, twisting the silver ring.

"Pretty," he observed.

"Thanks." She smiled. "The ring was my mother's."

"Is she in your life?"

A lengthy pause followed. Nora sobered, the smile gone from her features. "I wish I could say yes. The truth is, my mother and father died in a car accident not long after I left Cherish. The ring was her gift to me on my eighteenth birthday."

He studied Nora's classic profile, her high cheekbones and flawless skin. "When did you last speak to your mother?"

"We talked on the phone after I left, but not often. The conversations were brief and stilted. I never told them I was pregnant." Tears brimmed in her glorious eyes. "They never met their granddaughter."

"They never saw Samantha before they died?"

She flinched. "No."

"It must be hard. Sorrow and mourning. I wish I had the right words, though I'm truly sorry for your loss."

"Thank you." She nodded and didn't say more.

This was a discussion she obviously didn't want to broach.

Direct me, Lord, he prayed. *I won't dwell on a distressing topic that brings her pain.*

An emptiness settled in the pit of his stomach. If she felt comfortable, they could talk again. For now, he steered the conversation toward a lightheartedness while respecting her sadness.

As they exchanged pleasantries, he reached over and tucked a rebellious strand of her hair behind her ear. "We'll dine at a local establishment," he said. "Any suggestions?"

"I indulged in many BLTs at The Garden Terrace when I lived here. Plus, they serve the best mesquite barbecued ribs and sugar-free lemon cake. I drove by yesterday, and they're still open after all these years." Her gaze brightened. "They sponsor a local band every weekend."

"Ideal. A good meal and music. Shall we plan for seven o'clock on Friday evening?"

Her upturned gaze met his. "I'll check with Tom to be sure I'm not scheduled to work. If he gives the okay, then yes."

"Call me old-fashioned, but I insist on treating. Deal?"

"I call it chivalrous and generous."

"Deal, then?"

"Deal."

Immensely cheered by her response, Julian perked up.

She'd accepted his invitation. He waited for his pulse to

level off and considered his next words. He'd dated women in many cities and wasn't known for wearing his heart on his sleeve. However, with Nora the stakes were higher.

His fingers grazed her graceful chin. "I'd love to spend more time with you." He'd never made such a heartfelt declaration to any woman.

"Me too," she replied.

The moment was special. If he didn't reach out and take hold, it would disappear.

He leaned forward and brushed his lips on hers. It was all the encouragement she needed, because the kiss deepened. Soft, delicate, and delicious. For a few seconds, the squirrels stopped chattering, the wispy breeze paused, the snippets of conversation from a couple strolling by ceased. All that mattered was Nora and the delectable wave of emotion heading straight for his heart.

She placed her hands on his chest. "Julian, we're sitting outside on a porch."

"Yes, and the kiss was amazing."

"You're leaving. I'm leaving."

Truth prodded the recesses of his brain.

She was right. This was correct. He was going to lose her, lose *this*.

His chest pinched. He managed a smile. "Then let's treasure the days we have together and not analyze anything."

Her sweet smile reminded him that every moment in Cherish was special. Especially if the beautiful Nora was by his side.

CHAPTER 4

*T*he other members of Julian's team—a man and two women—were able to catch their train, and a measured commotion heralded their arrival.

Perched behind the front desk in the lobby, Nora checked them in. Amidst a round of laughter, they regaled Julian with hilarious stories about their travel mishaps. All three had taken the train into Cherish Central station directly from Atlanta.

Julian introduced them to Nora, and she welcomed them with a radiant smile.

Already, he missed their rapport from a few hours earlier. He ran their conversation through his mind and grinned, recalling her crooked smile when he'd referred to the Cherish area as delightful.

He noted her competence and courtesy. She remembered everyone's names and offered to carry their bags to their rooms. Julian quickly intervened, despite Nora's protests.

No bellboy, he mused as he lugged a third set of designer suitcases up two flights of stairs. No elevator, either. Wasn't Tom aware they were living in the twenty-first century?

Moreover, where *was* Tom? Julian had overheard Louise, who divided her time between housekeeping duties and keeping a watch on the staff, complain to Nora before lunch that despite his recent heart attack, Tom refused to follow his doctor's orders to rest. Apparently, Tom insisted on a hands-on approach, and Julian had already seen how Louise fussed over him, overly protective of his welfare.

When Julian finished carrying suitcases and escorting his team to their respective rooms, they all agreed to meet at the restaurant at six for dinner. Back downstairs, he looked around for Nora, finding her in the dining room setting the tables. His smile was enormous and completely over-the-top whenever he looked at her, yet he couldn't help himself.

He settled in the parlor with his laptop, pretending to work when he was really watching for any glimpse of Nora. She seemed in constant motion, tending to other guests as they arrived, answering the phone, running the vacuum over the carpet in the hall.

She worked too hard. She worked too much.

And the same question arose. Why? Were Tom and Nora related? If not, what was the connection? Judging by her frowns, her daughter didn't want to be there.

An image of the pretty teen, her mischievous smile when she thought no one was watching, her large ice-blue eyes and abundance of earrings, came to mind. Surely there was more to her than her outward, moody appearance. Was this typical adolescent rebellion?

He'd acted out in his teens. His mother hadn't taken an interest in him until his battle with alcohol surfaced.

Her neglect had fostered an outsized longing in Julian to be accepted, which ultimately had contributed to his alcohol abuse. It wasn't his mother's fault. He loved her, she'd made an effort, and he accepted full responsibility for his actions. His father had died when Julian and his brother were young,

41

and he had no real recollection of him. Only his mother, who'd hung on to her resentment of being a young widow for years.

Nora had become a single mother too soon as well.

Nora again. She was a treasure, comparable to a spray of sunflowers, spreading sunshine wherever she went. From what he'd observed, Samantha was foremost in Nora's heart.

Behind Samantha's petulant expression lay a promise of the beauty God had bequeathed to Nora. Surely, she had hidden talents and interests, and her spirit could be influenced by kindness. That is, if he could reach her, because she was as approachable as a prickly pear.

In his remaining days in Cherish, he wanted to get to know her better. After all, he was taking Nora out to dinner, so he was also interested in Samantha and how she might feel about him dating her mother.

One dinner is not a date, he repeated to himself.

Because his job required him to travel from city to city, he'd concluded long ago that he should remain single. He'd tried long-distance relationships, though the last break-up had been so hurtful for him and the woman, he'd never even returned to the city where she lived. Who would want a husband who was never around?

Indeed, he loved children and mentoring.

Was it enough? He'd been content. A bachelor's life with no strings ...

But still ...

Earlier, before his team arrived, Julian had run into Nora after he'd eaten a delectable lunch in the restaurant. He had asked if she liked music.

"Very much," she answered.

"There's a music store a ten-minute walking distance from here called Musically Yours," he said, watching as she arranged fragrant pink roses in a vase in the front hall. "I understand that thanks to the owner, Cherish boasts more world-renowned musicians and performers per square mile than any place south of Manhattan. Her husband is Ryan Edwards. I don't listen to opera, but even *I've* heard of Ryan Edwards."

"Opera singers' voices are so elegant," Nora replied. "My father tuned in to the Metropolitan Opera broadcast on the radio every Saturday. But I've already been to Musically Yours. I stopped on my way to the farmer's market this morning and met Dorothy Edwards, the owner, and she is lovely. Then I went back an hour ago and bought a guitar."

Julian stared at her. "You bought a guitar?"

She smiled. "Yes, for Samantha."

"She'll be taking lessons while she's here?"

"She prefers online instruction. Everything seems to be virtual nowadays, so I didn't object."

"You can't learn guitar in an afternoon."

"I'm sure Samantha realizes that."

"Can she read music?"

"No." Nora turned away from the vase, massaging her temples. "I'm encouraging her. Otherwise, she's glued to her phone."

A computer isn't much better, Julian wanted to say.

He kept silent. He recalled Nora's sharp rebuttal about judging another person's parenting skills when he had no children of his own.

Perhaps music could become common ground for him and Samantha. Though Julian wasn't a musician, he'd heard that Joseph Slater, a renowned worship artist and musician, lived in Cherish, and participated in the worship music ministry at the church.

Julian had made peace by welcoming God into his life,

and he prayed for the same peace for Samantha and Nora. A love of music might spark Samantha's interest to listen to worship songs and thus lead her and her mother on a church-attending path.

One could only hope, he thought. One could only pray.

*H*ours later, Julian gave up on pretending to work and headed to the lounge to wait for his team. He noticed Tom sitting alone, nursing a glass of wine. Julian asked for a glass of soda water and then weaved around the tables to join him. He intended to ask Tom about Nora. Who knew better about her stay than Tom?

With a genial smile, he gripped the back of an empty stool and greeted him. "We briefly chatted yesterday. You may remember I'm Julian Wilson."

Tom's gaze narrowed. "Course I remember. You're from the Fresh 'n' Good chain."

"I trust you've read our five-star reviews."

"I've read the criticisms."

"If I can be of any help, let me know," Julian said. "I have a lot of experience running restaurants."

"So do I. Your company lacks a certain something."

Julian suppressed a smile at Tom's outward distaste of the chain. "Such as?"

"Personal interest in the patrons. I know everyone who eats at my restaurant. I understand their lives, their interests, and even their pets. Can you say the same?"

"No. I can't." Julian was used to giving orders. Perhaps he should listen more to people like Tom—an entrepreneur with a boatload of wisdom and experience.

The men exchanged a brief handshake.

"You have a fine place here," Julian said.

"Yep." Tom cast a critical eye at the bartender engaged in

a heated conversation with a customer while another unsuccessfully tried to signal him. Then Tom's gaze traveled to Louise, who had entered the lounge. She caught his attention, and he grinned, giving her a head-to-toe stare.

"May I join you?" Julian held onto his glass, not positive he should set it on the table.

"For a while." Tom peered at his watch, then acknowledged the stool across from him. "I'm due to duck into the dining room soon."

"I won't keep you." Julian slipped onto the vacant stool. "I wished to compliment you on the well-prepared dinner I enjoyed last evening. Your chef is outstanding."

"Yep."

"Nora was my waitress."

"Yep."

"She's efficient," Julian confirmed. *And wonderful.*

"Uh, huh." Tom came straight and rigid on his stool.

Rifling in his mind for how he'd given offense, Julian came to the assumption that his praises were too feeble.

"She's excellent and efficient." He hastily sifted through his declaration. "Outstanding."

Tom slid the stool back. "Nora is an old hand at innkeeping."

"How fortunate." Julian intended to fasten onto Tom's every word. "Is she your relative?"

No answer.

"I'm needed in the dining room." With a grunt, Tom rose, threw Julian an abrupt nod, and turned on his heels. Louise also headed to the dining room as Julian's party started toward him. He took a last gulp of his drink and hailed them.

Tom ushered the foursome into the restaurant, where mouthwatering scents of chicken and dumplings tempted Julian's nostrils. It was dinner hour and conversation bubbled.

Each table was covered with a paisley tablecloth, a pink rosebud in a golden-flecked vase placed at the center. Tiny tea lights and tapered candles burned with welcoming flickers, and Julian took note of the steps taken to create a hospitable atmosphere. He imagined savoring numerous meals in this friendly community, shopping the farmer's market with Nora and Samantha, and attending church services together.

A fantasy, not a reality.

The admonition brought a clench to his chest. He might be staying in Cherish for a few months. Nora wasn't. And he certainly wouldn't have time to learn any of his restaurant's patrons by name.

"Julian. Hello! We meet again."

Julian swiveled at the sound of a familiar male voice, and a man sporting a bow tie waved. He sat at a table with two women and another man.

"Hi." Julian strode over as Tom seated Julian's team nearby.

"Maxwell Archer. Call me Max." Max rose and performed formal introductions. "The resident bird-watcher, at your service."

"You're joking."

"About my name?"

"About being the resident bird-watcher."

"I never joke about my birds." Max drummed his fingers on his legs. "Those colorful creatures bring a sparkle to my days. Besides my wife, obviously."

The dark-haired woman next to him smiled and ducked her head. The others laughed.

"Did I miss something?" Julian asked.

"Join us on a bird-watching hike sometime," the woman said. "The hike will explain an hour's worth of conversation."

"I'm Julian Wilson." Julian shook hands with Max. "I don't own birds or dogs. I run restaurants."

Max adjusted his bow tie. "We were wondering why you were in Cherish."

"My coworkers and I work for Fresh 'n' Good." Julian gestured to the table where they sat. "We're scouting the area because the chain may open a restaurant here." A stab of guilt reminded him of his assurance to Nora—that the eatery he oversaw wouldn't drive any local place out of business. He touched the base of his neck and prayed for guidance to steer the owners toward becoming an asset to the community, not a hindrance.

"By the way, Max," Julian asked, shuffling backward, "did you catch your dogs?"

Max patted his shirt pocket. "There's invariably a mishap when those dogs run loose. Happily, bacon treats are the key." He beamed at the woman beside him. "Allow me to introduce my beautiful wife, Sarah. Across from us is Sheriff Nicholas Thompson and his wife, Emmanuelle."

A tall blond-haired man was already on his feet. "If I can be of assistance, Julian, please holler."

"Nicholas is an integral part of our local law enforcement," Max put in. "He spends his days enforcing the law, and his dog, Molly Belle, spends her days racing up and down every block and breaking the law."

A collective sigh of agreement came from both wives.

"Molly Belle is a handful," Nicholas admitted. "But many golden retrievers are energetic."

"Energetic?" Tom approached the table. "Why, I still remember when you brought her into the inn and she knocked over a crystal vase filled with roses. There was water and broken glass everywhere."

"You banned Molly Belle from ever entering your establishment again," Nicholas reminded.

"With excellent reason." Tom scratched his whiskered chin. "Take Molly Belle to Frank's Pizza, instead. They offer outdoor accommodations there."

"Anywhere except here," Nicholas muttered. "Is that what you're saying?"

"You got that right." Tom turned to Max. "My ban also includes Tiny Tim."

Julian let the relief sink in. He wouldn't be forced to encounter a small dog.

Max waved Tom's reference aside. "Why? He's only a puppy and eager to please." Max's obvious bewilderment at how anyone could doubt his dog's character brought a glimmer of amusement to Tom's eyes.

Laughter filled the silence after a few seconds, then everyone talked at once.

Special friends, Julian thought. Citizens creating experiences, building each other up in a tight-knit community. He wished for a close connection with people, yet he'd pushed his wishes into the background while a successful career propelled him ever forward. He told himself moving from place to place suited him. It was the way he'd grown up, and the only life he'd ever known.

He said good-bye to the friends and joined his team members. As he sat, he scanned the dining area for Nora.

A while later, she entered and didn't notice him.

His mouth opened in surprise as Samantha followed her, wearing an apron over a pair of slim-fitting jeans and a peach-colored blouse. Cheerily, he waved, and she reciprocated with a tentative smile.

Much to his dismay, neither Samantha nor her mother waitressed his table. When coffee was served bitter once again, he frowned into its contents.

. . .

*D*usk had fallen by the time Nora finished computing bills, collecting payments, and checking room availability.

As the dining room had filled, she'd noticed several locals had reserved tables. Soon, Louise and Tom approached her in the lobby.

"Can you and Samantha waitress?" Louise asked. "We're short-staffed again."

Excuses poured out of Nora—her presence was required at the reception desk, the parlor cried out for a tidying, the laundry attendant complained it was impossible to keep up with the demand for clean linens.

"A job will keep Samantha busy." Louise softened her tone and tapped a finger to her temple. "She's a smart girl."

"She's only fifteen. Isn't she too young for waitressing?" Nora refuted. "I presumed Tom wouldn't hire her."

"I'm not hiring her," Tom reminded her. "She's working for free in exchange for room and board. Besides, you insisted on offering your tips to the Boys and Girls center, and I assume Samantha will do the same."

Her parents had continuously donated extra linens and supplies to the various shelters in the community. It was the least Nora could do.

"Perhaps several hours of training for Samantha first ..." she began.

"On-the-job experience is the greatest kind." He and Louise gave identical nods.

"Tom is brilliant." Louise touched his upper arm and smiled.

Tom wrapped up the discussion by blowing out a labored breath. He sagged against the doorway, which unwittingly prompted Nora into action. Louise fixed his shirt collar and volunteered to walk him to his suite as Nora hurried off.

She climbed the stairs to her room and quickly showered. Then she cast an appraisal in the mirror over her clean turquoise blouse, tailored honey-colored slacks, and leather loafers. A quick swipe of mascara and pink lip gloss completed her makeup routine. She styled her hair in an orderly bun.

Mentally, she rehearsed her approach as she knocked on Samantha's bedroom door, sending a plea to the heavens for serenity. She wasn't prepared for an argument.

"Come in. The door's unlocked," Samantha called out.

A guitar was balanced on her lap, and her computer screen displayed an instructional YouTube video featuring a soft-spoken teen playing a guitar. Her phone was open beside her.

Nora stepped farther into the room. "Did you learn a lot today?"

"I'm reading tablature. Basic chords are next and then strumming patterns."

"You're off to a fine start." Nora tilted her head toward Samantha's cellphone. "Who are you texting?"

"My boyfriend."

"Edison is learning guitar too?"

Samantha sighed as if Nora had just asked if her boyfriend had three heads. "He's interested in music and is a proficient guitarist. He's forming a band and asked me to join."

"Tell him good luck and good-bye, honey. We're needed downstairs. The restaurant is full to the rafters with diners."

Samantha's complexion turned colorless. "Now?"

"Now."

Samantha's thumbs flew across her phone's keyboard, then she snapped it shut. "There's a weak internet signal here, anyway."

"Oh well," Nora countered cheerfully.

"I really want to learn how to play the guitar."

"I applaud your efforts, Samantha, but Rome wasn't built in a day."

"What does that mean?"

"It means patience is a virtue, and time is required to accomplish greatness."

"Can I ask you a question, Mom?"

"Certainly."

"Why are we really here in Cherish?" Samantha set the guitar beside her.

"Your grandparents once owned this inn."

"You've told me that a hundred times."

"I owe them this—a tribute to all their effort. When I learned Tom was ill, I reached out to him."

"How were they—Grandma and Grandpa? I mean, I've seen pictures."

"They were wonderful and moral people." Tears pricked Nora's eyes. "Reliable, conscientious and loving."

"I never met them."

"Sadly, no."

"I think about them a lot." Samantha drew a wobbly breath. "I've prayed to God, but He hasn't given me any answers."

"Prayed about what?"

"What I can really do in my life to make a difference, so Grandma and Grandpa would be proud of me."

"You're at the in-between stage. It's not up to you to figure the world out at fifteen." Nora placed an encouraging hand on her daughter's shoulder. "I'm in my thirties and I'm still not sure. I can only try my best."

Nora had never understood a God who didn't respond to prayers. How could He take her parents, Samantha's grandparents, away from them?

Correction. Nora had deserted her parents when they needed her most. Not God.

She'd listened to sermons about a person's days already being written in God's book. Her heartache ran deep because of her faulty resolutions.

She offered an inward prayer—*Help me, Lord, to advise Samantha to follow the right path*—and felt lighter for the asking, as if a boulder had been heaved from her chest.

She wasn't forced to raise her daughter alone. God would assist her, and she shouldn't drive Him from the picture. His blessings were significant and meant to be embraced.

How? She prided herself on being a self-sufficient, independent woman. Or was she stalled in a version that wasn't truly her? Independence was noble, but wasn't it still okay to rely on someone else? To have a partner to share life with?

"*Guide Samantha to find worth in what is true*," Julian had advised. "*Stay the course and belie*ve."

Her heart gravitated toward him. He was a decent, honest man who truly loved God. His words brought hope.

"Perhaps," she said to her daughter, "we'll go to services at Memorial Street Church. I attended every Sunday when I was in elementary school."

Samantha smiled, dimples prominent, despite the apprehension shadowing her features.

Nora drew in a breath. "Did you wish to discuss your prayers?"

"Some other time." Samantha surged to her feet. "Give me a moment to change."

"Okay," Nora said. "I'm here whenever you want to talk."

Ten minutes later, mother and daughter descended the stairs to the lobby.

"Last night the dining room was almost empty, except for the guy you kept smiling at," Samantha observed. "You drenched him with a jug of water. Remember?"

"A glass of water, not a jug, and he didn't get wet," Nora corrected.

They reported to the kitchen, and Nora donned the inn's trademark red apron.

Samantha did the same, then clutched her hands together. "I've never waitressed before. Louise and Tom know that, right?"

"They have complete faith in you, as do I. An exemplary waitress is cordial, attentive to the customer, and quick," Nora explained. "A thorough knowledge of the menu is helpful, so let's review tonight's offerings."

"I studied the menu last night," Samantha said. "Has anything changed?"

"This evening's special is roasted chicken with dumplings. The recipe was given to Louise by a young woman named Crissy and is a favorite dish here."

Samantha zipped over to a cook and plied him with questions, then inspected the plated entrees ready to be delivered to the dining room. The cook forked a serving of chicken onto a plate, and Samantha took a bite. She chewed for several seconds, then swallowed.

"Flavorful and moist," she declared. "I can taste the rosemary."

"Flavorful? Rosemary?" Nora blankly echoed. She didn't think her daughter even knew what rosemary was.

"Mom, can't you taste it?" Samantha asked.

"I haven't had time to eat." Nora realized she must still be grinning like a court jester. Her daughter was displaying an interest in food other than pizza and potato chips.

"Always sample the specials," another server said, pausing in the doorway. "Then you can honestly recommend the dishes."

"I watch the food channel on my phone sometimes."

Samantha piled dumplings onto her plate. "Though I'm not sure if I'll be a good waitress."

Nora patted her daughter's arm. "If you ever finish eating, you'll be sure to wow all the diners."

Moments later, the twosome emerged from the kitchen. Nora's posture was strong, her gait wide. Samantha's shoulders slumped as she walked to her first assigned table.

And then an amazing thing happened.

To Nora's astonishment, Samantha proved skillful at waitressing. Her chest filled with pride at her daughter's charm and grace as she chatted up the diners and recommended Crissy's chicken and dumplings. She'd shed her sulkiness and wasn't clumsy at all.

With a silent chuckle, Nora applauded this small step forward in her daughter's growth.

As she refilled wine glasses for an elderly couple, she identified Julian's voice before she saw him.

She turned.

He'd been watching her, and his gaze drifted appreciatively to her face.

Her cheeks burned—embarrassed he'd seen her again out of her element. He looked drop-dead gorgeous in a pristine white pressed shirt that emphasized his broad shoulders. Black dress pants fit his long legs to perfection. He grinned his approval toward Samantha, then returned his gaze to Nora.

"You're enchanting," he mouthed.

"Another pickup line," she mouthed back. "But thank you."

When he turned to his team members, she lingered to listen in awe as he carried off a clear description of the area, then noted his keen attention when one of the others spoke. He was so at ease around people, so poised. He knew just what to say and when to say it. She'd always been quiet and a bit shy.

A harried server approached, reminding that the elderly couple had inquired about their meal. Another server brushed by, whispering that they were running low on chicken, and thus the night's special would soon run out. Nora hurried to the kitchen for the couple's dinner, then apologized to them for the wait and promised free desserts of their choice.

The pressures of the long day and evening soon left their mark, and Nora dreamed of soaking in an inviting bubble bath and reading a riveting romance novel when she finally was able to relax in her room. By the time most of the diners had left, save for some stragglers, she felt like she'd switched to autopilot.

She didn't permit herself to look directly at Julian, not wanting the distraction.

Several times, though, she couldn't resist, and he caught her gaze and smiled.

My, that did odd things to her insides. Quickly she focused elsewhere. When she couldn't help herself, she chanced another glance in his direction. His gaze was always on her.

The meaning in his eyes—desire, a magnetic attraction beyond rationalization, caused her pulse to speed to an alarming rate.

Stop acting as if you're a besotted schoolgirl, she reprimanded herself as she replenished drinks. She should be grateful he'd only be in Cherish a while. When she passed his table a final time, she hid a yawn with her fingers. Her knees wobbled, and she braced a hand on the wall to steady herself.

"Nora?"

His concerned voice came from behind her. She spun. He was only within a few inches from her.

"You're exhausted, Cinderella," he said. "Your day has been filled with work, work, work."

"I've been on my feet a long while tonight." She extended a trivializing wave, fearful he might feel sorry for her. "I should've changed my shoes and worn sneakers instead of loafers."

He fetched a chair. "Please sit down."

"I can't. There are tables to clear and—"

"Please." He gently placed his hands on her shoulders.

With a resigned smile, she sank into the chair. She longed to kick off her shoes and soak her aching feet.

"You and your daughter were brilliant tonight," he said.

"Thanks." She looked around the near-empty dining room. "Where is she?"

"In the kitchen."

"She's probably scouring the counters for leftover dumplings."

"More nutritious than potato chips?" He brought on his devastating smile.

She grinned. "Absolutely."

"Are you all right?"

"Certainly."

"You look tired."

"That's not a very complimentary thing to say to a woman."

"I'm sorry. You're gorgeous, though slightly pale."

"In truth, I'm exhausted." She blew a stray strand of hair from her face. She must look a sight with her bun coming undone and the little makeup she'd applied long faded.

"I'll finish for you."

"By waitressing?"

"I'm a restaurant man. I've served in every capacity from busboy to concierge."

"You've assisted in the kitchen too?"

"I try. I'm not much of a cook, though."

"What's your specialty?"

"Toast."

She chuckled. She enjoyed his witty sense of humor. He thought quick, whereas it took her forever to think of a humorous response.

"Now you're a top manager who calls all the shots," she said.

"Touché." He tipped his head back and laughed, a rich throaty chuckle. But then his laughter was replaced by a burning intensity in his eyes. "I'm looking forward to seeing you on Friday evening."

"You're seeing me right now." She stretched out her legs. "We're both staying here, so I assume we'll bump into each other often."

"Your assumption suits me perfectly."

She peeked over at the table where he and his team had dined. The others were gone. When had they left? All her concentration had been focused on Julian.

He cupped her chin. "Please promise me you'll get some rest." His deep velvety tone wrapped around her.

"I promise."

"Have you eaten?"

Her forehead throbbed. She rubbed her temples. "No."

"Will Tom and Louise mind if I sneak into the kitchen?"

"They left earlier. Together, naturally." Nora wiggled her eyebrows. "I'm certain it's okay."

"I'll fix you a plate to bring to your room." He strode to the kitchen and returned with a container and plastic utensils. Samantha trotted beside him, amiable yet reserved.

Julian was kind and considerate, all traits Nora admired in a man. He also harbored a profound religious faith, which he openly shared.

She recalled a Psalm, 37:23, which she'd memorized as a child. "The steps of a good man are ordered by the Lord."

Plus, Samantha seemed to like Julian, at least a little.

"Your waitressing was outstanding tonight," Nora congratulated her daughter.

"Thanks, Mom." Samantha shrugged indifferently, trying to act as if the praise didn't affect her. "I think Grandma and Grandpa would be proud."

Nora's heart melted. "Very proud, indeed. Both of your grandparents had high expectations and were sticklers for excellence. You were utter perfection."

Samantha's forehead creased. "Is perfection an admirable trait?"

"Definitely," Julian said. "Reach for the stars and never underestimate yourself."

"Well, I'm off to my room." With a wide grin, Samantha yanked off her apron, snatched up her takeout container, and left with the easy, breezy gait of youth. Her hips and delicate waist were filling out more each day.

Outwardly, Nora smiled. Inwardly, she questioned herself.

She swung in the opposite direction from her parents when it came to rearing her daughter. She wanted to allow Samantha the freedom to express herself. But perhaps there was a middle ground. Mistakes. Corrections. Dust yourself off and try again.

Wasn't that the definition of life's cycle? Compromises. In Nora's case, she incessantly confronted the same challenges and insecurities in different seasons of her life.

She wasn't worthy to receive God's grace at eighteen. She wasn't worthy at thirty-three.

"Your daughter is enchanting," Julian was saying.

"I agree. Thanks."

It seemed as if all Nora did was thank him.

The jaded side of her interrupted. Was Julian's thought-fulness one-sided? Was he putting on a show for his team by acting interested in Nora's welfare?

No. It couldn't be.

Her ex had professed undying love and vowed to care for her and their daughter. Alas, both were fleeting traits of a teenage boy who'd married her on a whim—the exhilaration of juvenile infatuation. Love was more than that. It had to be.

Julian was mature. His actions were sincere and heartfelt.

He settled on a chair beside her. His gray eyes, soft as a pencil drawing, drew her to him. The woodsy scent of his aftershave sent her senses into turmoil.

She couldn't remember afterward if she'd stopped breathing.

His lips grazed her ear. "I didn't see you nearly as much as I'd hoped this evening."

"Clearly you observed the dining room was filled to capacity."

He leaned closer.

Her lips parted and her heart did a double flip. Surely he wouldn't kiss her in the restaurant. Pleasure swept through her at the thought of him wrapping his arms around her. Kissing her as she clung to his muscular frame.

Could she be falling for him despite her misgivings?

Certainly not. She wouldn't jeopardize her heart with a long-distance romance. She was years past being a foolish adolescent.

The romantic, fancy-free half of her brain was thrilled he'd arranged their Friday night date. Nevertheless, the reasonable and sensible half chattered on about their two different lives and two different universes.

She should've told him her days were too hectic. She should've refused his offer.

She hadn't.

Looking back at her life as the pounds piled on, she'd harbored resentment and hurt until they had almost broken her. But in the end, those same conflicts brought her strength.

A win, to be sure.

However, her anguish over her dissolved marriage had led to wariness, and one of the hardest things to shake off was distrust. Her goal was to make it on her own. She didn't depend on anyone.

Still, was Julian the man she'd been searching for her entire life?

CHAPTER 5

*S*everal days passed quickly.

Despite the fact that Nora recommended that Tom recuperate in his upstairs suite, he was invariably within a few feet of her. Today, on the first Saturday of her month-long stay in Cherish, he'd finally agreed to rest.

Pencil in hand, Nora sat at a rosewood writing desk in his private office. He preferred handwritten documents rather than a computer because pencil and paper were convenient and readily accessible. She tugged open a drawer and rummaged through stacks of billing, seeking the current month's invoices. Unable to locate anything, she set down the pencil. Her mind immediately gravitated to her date with Julian the previous evening.

He'd been polite, gentlemanly, and oh-so-considerate.

He'd met her in the Cherish Hills Inn lobby promptly at six thirty, allowing them ample time to get to the restaurant. Earlier in the week he'd requested her cellphone number, texting each evening to inquire about her day and wishing her sweet dreams. Each time his name crossed her phone screen, her spirits soared.

He was attentive and thoughtful. She'd never been with a man who held such consideration for her, and she appreciated his attention.

For their date, she'd chosen a flirty, pale-green chiffon dress, strappy sandals, and a chocolate-brown leather clutch rather than her everyday handbag. She gathered a silky, sea-green scarf around her shoulders in case the night was chilly.

As she descended the stairs to the lobby, her pulse fluttered in excitement when she saw him. He closed the distance between them in two long strides.

"Good evening, Nora. You are gorgeous." He greeted her with his customary warm smile and admiring appraisal.

Nora bit back a smile. He'd complimented her more in a few days than her ex had during their entire relationship. Julian was amazing.

"Thanks." Her fingers welcomed his soothing grip. "Though you always say that."

"Because I tell the truth." He held her gaze. His eyes were a deep, smoky gray. Purposeful, earnest, and comforting.

Instinctively, she held in her stomach. She'd forgotten to pack shapewear for the trip. And then she thought, *No worries*. This was Julian, and he seemed to appreciate her no matter her size.

He captured her hands in his. "The opportunity to go out with you tonight is a special gift."

"We've seen each other all week," she reminded.

"With constant interruptions. This night is ours and ours alone."

As guests passed, they stood in the lobby holding hands.

He didn't let go. Neither did she.

His almond-brown polo shirt and tan pants emphasized his magnificent, all-male physique, and her heart lurched. Oh, and his wonderful smile.

"Is Samantha taking a virtual guitar lesson tonight?" he asked.

"Tom bulldozed her into waitressing again." Nora inclined her head toward the dining room. "For me, a win-win. I won't worry about her. Bonus—she'll eat a hearty, nutritious meal."

"Good on both counts." Julian placed a casual arm around her shoulders. "The Garden Terrace is only a couple streets over. Shall we walk?"

"I was going to suggest the same."

He ushered her to the doorway. "See?"

"See what?"

"We're already clicking because we're reading each other's minds."

She laughed, the chiffon swirling around her as they descended the stairway. Her limbs were light, her soul carefree. The fragrance of spicy-sweet summer blossoms, the promise of gladness, nurtured every thread of her being.

A breeze grabbed a lock of Julian's hair, and she stilled the impulse to push it back with her fingers. The setting sun highlighted the natural mahogany hue, reminding her of the finest, shiny wood. Her heartbeat thudded louder, and it took a great deal of effort not to stare at him.

When they arrived at The Garden Terrace, he escorted her inside. Mesquite barbecued ribs beckoned. She sniffed, savoring the scrumptious smells.

He'd made reservations, though she'd assured him it wasn't necessary.

She was wrong. The place was packed. Waitresses scurried by with dish after dish of brisket and fried onions, and the chatter of diners pervaded every inch of the space. Yet it all faded into the background as Julian kept his fingers laced through hers.

"This place may lack sophistication, but the down-home food is delicious," she said.

His lips curved into a playful grin while he regarded the wood-beamed ceiling. "I'd hoped for a more romantic atmosphere."

Romantic. Julian was a romantic. He probably was the sort of man to send flowers and pick out distinctive gold foil cards. Blank cards so he could handwrite a message.

Besides his chivalrous manner, there was no mistaking the expression on his face when he looked at her. A deep affection was growing and more than a passing interest.

The feeling was mutual. She grinned back at the man she was beginning to fall for.

Julian flashed a smile to a couple sitting at a table near the stage. Their curious gazes had swiveled to him and Nora.

"Who are they?" Nora asked.

"Nicholas, the town sheriff, and his wife, Emmanuelle."

"You've been here less than a week," Nora said, "yet you know more folks than me."

"And Max is the guy who chased after the two dogs at the farmer's market."

"The big dog and the cute tiny dog?"

"Right." Visibly, Julian shivered.

"What's wrong?"

He shrugged. "Not a thing."

"Don't you like dogs?"

"Big dogs, sure." His eyebrows drew together. "Little dogs, not so much. Someday I'll explain my phobia."

Julian had a phobia? And when would he tell her? He was leaving soon.

"Who is Max?" she asked instead.

"He's the fellow on stage wearing a bow tie and playing the harmonica. That's his wife, Sarah, standing over there, and her uncle Gerry is half of this band. Max is the other half, and I understand their band's name is"—Julian peered at the sign by the stage—"The Bearded June Bugs. I overheard someone saying they change their name with the seasons."

"I can hardly keep track of my own name, let alone change it," Nora said.

"Likewise." Julian nodded agreement. "Initially, I had Cherish pegged as a sleepy little town."

"If I remember correctly, you described the area as delightful."

He offered a lopsided grin.

"Other observations?" she asked.

"Two more words. Flawless and special." His gray eyes shimmered. "Like you."

Flawless. Special.

She focused on his words, and her heartbeat sounded in her ears.

He drew her hand through his arm and led her to Nicholas' table to exchange introductions. Nicholas and Emmanuelle were both strikingly attractive. Each had blond hair, and they extended generous, welcoming smiles.

Nicholas' deep blue eyes sparkled with perceptiveness as he remarked to Julian, "And this lovely woman is …?" He winked, and they all chuckled. Apparently, the rumor wind-mill was already spinning. "Didn't she waitress at the Cherish Hills Inn the other night?"

Nora extended a hand. "I'm Nora Lancaster. Tom has been sick and I'm here from Virginia to help him."

"You are friends?"

"A fair description. My parents once owned the inn."

Julian's sharp gaze landed on her. She avoided it.

"A pleasure to meet you." Nicholas shook her hand. "Wel-come back to Cherish."

"Such a great town. My daughter agrees."

At least Nora hoped Samantha agreed. It was too soon to tell since the teen changed her moods with the wind.

"Nora's daughter is the competent young woman who also waitressed tables when you dined at the inn," Julian clarified. "Cheers to her lovely mother. Anyone can see she's doing a fine job raising her daughter."

Nora glanced up, surprised to see the expression of pride on Julian's face.

"Samantha was our waitress," Emmanuelle chimed in. "She told me she's learning how to play the guitar online, and I congratulated her. I'm a harpist and teach lessons at Musically Yours. I told her if she ever wanted formal instruction to read music, I'm available."

"This is a wonderfully artistic community," Nora said.

"We wouldn't live anywhere else." Nicholas drew an arm around his wife. "Tight-knit and caring, our Christian fellowship will support you through life's rough patches."

Emmanuelle's observant gaze lingered on Nora. "Can we expect to see you both in church on Sunday morning? Ryan and Dorothy, the owners of Musically Yours, direct the worship music, and our illustrious duo"—Emmanuelle gestured to the stage—"sing in the choir."

"Not everyone in town is musical," Nicholas piped in. "We sit in our favorite pew in the front row, listen to an outstanding sermon, and I sing my heart out, albeit out of tune, to all the hymns."

"You're describing me," Julian agreed.

There was a lull in the conversation and Nora stared at the deer antlers mounted above Nicholas. This was the part where these decent faith-filled people expected her to declare that she would attend church.

She grappled with a suitable reply before opting for the

truth. "Neither Samantha nor I have attended services in years."

I'm not sure why God wants someone like me, she thought. *I've been married, divorced, and my mistakes are too numerous to count.*

Aloud, she managed, "I suppose I'm a work in progress."

Julian tightened his grip on her hand. "God will meet you wherever you are." With that, he bade Emmanuelle and Nicholas to enjoy their meal.

Nora and Julian followed a server to a cozy booth in a secluded corner.

Nora loved it all. Their bantering while they dined on bacon-wrapped mushrooms—one of her favorites, she told him. The chaotic clattering of dishes, the laughter that went on for hours.

They'd each finished a plate of sticky barbecued ribs, twisting the bone apart and feasting on both sides, then wiping their hands on numerous napkins while downing glasses of cold, sweet tea. Max's band played a classic 80s rock song, and she and Julian sang along with the chorus.

"My favorite music era," Julian declared. "Who doesn't love 'Free Fallin'?"

"Or 'Born in the USA,'" Nora agreed with a laugh.

When she declined the specialty sugar-free lemon cake, Julian offered an indulgent smile. "There's always room for dessert," he encouraged.

She patted her stomach. "I eat my fair share, believe me."

"What do you mean?"

"Julian, I'm not exactly a toothpick. I should lose a few pounds."

"You're kidding, right? I like a woman with curves."

"Uh, huh. Perhaps if there was a little less of a curve around my waist."

"Women are so ill-advised." He shook his head, his gaze

warming as he smiled at her. "I assume you lived here for many years."

"Right."

"What's your favorite remembrance of Cherish?"

"Hmm." She paused at the unexpected question, admiring the way he'd deftly navigated the conversation away from her perceived faults. "I suppose when I was little, my remembrances were the same as any child. Carefree summers racing through a sprinkler on a sweltering day and pedaling to a bee farm on the edge of town with my friends."

"A bee farm?"

"The owner harvested and sold the honey, and his nephew baked homemade sourdough bread. In fact, my parents bought the honey and mixed it in tea for sore throats."

"I've done the same and drizzled honey on toast."

"And pancakes."

"What else?

"Well." She rested her elbows on the table and leaned her chin in her hands. "I once had a winter adventure I'll never forget."

"Indeed?" The question was light, his tone cautious.

"I was ten years old." She settled in her seat. "It was a snow day, my parents were working at the inn, and my friends and I were swinging on a playground set in my back-yard. We were all bundled in hats and gloves and heavy coats."

She blew out a sigh.

"And then?"

"I got off the swing and accepted a dare."

He quirked an eyebrow.

"One friend dared me to touch the metal part of the swing with my tongue."

"Oh, no."

"Exactly."

"What did you do?"

"I brought the swing into my house with my tongue attached."

"What?" He laughed, the bottomless, throaty laugh she loved, and raised his hands in mock horror. They enjoyed the same sense of humor. A bit wry but always fun.

"So what did you do?" he asked.

She took a swallow of iced tea. "Do you want to know what was I *expected* to do or what actually happened?"

"I've heard you're supposed to be patient and your tongue will unfreeze itself."

"Correct."

"But …?"

"I tried to pull my tongue off, and it hurt." She concealed the fact she'd been near hysteria. "Fortunately, my friends ran to get a neighbor and she used warm water to thaw my tongue."

"You're mentioning friends and neighbors." He grabbed her hands, his thumbs massaging her palms. "No siblings?"

"I'm an only child. You?"

"My brother and his wife and kids live in Pennsylvania. We're a few hours from each other. I see him and my twin nieces whenever I can."

"I assume not often, considering your constant travel."

Julian gave a curt nod.

She closed her fingers around her glass of tea. She still felt the warmth of his thumbs on her skin. "Now that you've heard my story, what's your best childhood recollection?"

"The first day of school," he replied. "No matter what state we lived in, my mother always took a photo of my brother and me holding our bookbags and waiting for the school bus. She'd buy the bookbags at a local thrift store, and they weren't always in the best shape. Ripped, zippers wouldn't work, that sort of thing."

"Oh. I'm sorry."

He shrugged. "It's okay."

"Did you like school?" Nora asked.

"Some subjects, like English, and sports. Little League games on mild summer nights were fun."

"Lots of memories, both happy and sad," she mused. Few happy ones for her once she'd reached the difficult teen years, when she rebelled and questioned why she was constantly knee-deep in chores.

Even when they were done eating, they hung out at the restaurant for another two hours, chatting with townspeople as they passed, sharing their keenness for lyrics as Max's two-man band belted out familiar tunes.

When servers pointedly began clearing tables, Nora surveyed the near-empty restaurant. Most of the patrons were gone, and even the band had packed up.

She stood. "We'd better leave."

Julian paid the check and dropped a generous tip. "I'll walk you back to the inn."

"How chivalrous, considering you're going to the same place," she teased.

His hand lightly touched her back. "My pleasure, my lady."

Together, they exited. A restful June breeze washed over her, and Julian tucked her silk shawl closer around her shoulders. The moon flashed a sliver of silver, and a twinkle of stars blanketed the dark sky.

Dinner had been delectable, the iced tea refreshing.

The moonlight stroll with Julian, however, was exquisite.

In a matter of days, he'd become a good friend who happened to be staying in the same town. A happy coincidence. Serendipity. Nothing more.

Nevertheless, they'd become more than friends since they'd gotten to know each other.

No, no, no.

But then he smiled at her and slid his strong fingers through hers.

Okay, he was definitely more than a friend.

A lump formed in her throat at the realization that everything in this tranquil town—including spending time with Julian—would soon end. Her real-time existence in a crowded city, the exorbitant cost of living, cramped spaces and rush-hour traffic jams, tightened an anxious knot in her stomach.

"I'm getting tired of the rat race," she admitted softly.

"Which is?" he asked, his gaze expressive.

"Running myself ragged. My job in Richmond is satisfying, although the deadlines are taking a toll on my relationship with Samantha. She's left alone after school too often. She's responsible and an exemplary student, though I still worry."

"At my wise age of thirty-five, I've concluded that people make time for what's important to them. Perhaps electing to take shorter hours at your job might help?"

She bristled. "My boss depends on me. I'm not an entrepreneur who has the luxury of creating my own schedule."

"You're free to choose where, how, and when. Sometimes solid principles are shoved to the side by our will to succeed." He sighed. "I'm philosophizing, and my explanation is meant more for me than for you."

It was a quiet statement, and she accepted it in the manner in which it was intended—as an honest assessment of their lifestyles.

"What's important to you?" she asked.

"God and church, my mother, my brother and his family.

Oftentimes my priorities are out of whack because of my hectic calendar, though I've made certain my mother lives in her own home and is financially secure."

Nora nodded. This was Julian, always looking out for others. Kind and caring to his mother.

And he was right. She knew she shouldn't choose her job over spending time with her daughter. Guilt encompassed her like a veil of sadness, and her eyes misted.

"You're an amazing woman, Nora."

She blinked back tears. "I'm a single parent carrying all the expenses. Nonetheless, it's not a fair excuse."

"Fair to whom?"

"Fair to Samantha."

He stroked her cheek. No one had done that in such a long time, and she'd missed the closeness.

"I wish I could make your days easier," he said.

He did, by strolling with her, talking with her. Comforting her.

"Thank you." It was a relief to voice her feelings, realizing innately he'd never judge her. She reached up and touched his cheek before she realized the action was too familiar, too intimate. Hastily, she dropped her hand.

They neared the inn, and he stopped at the corner. Ever so gently, he snuggled her against his sturdy chest.

"I'm beginning to love this little town and everything in it." A glimmer of happiness lit his expression. "In addition, I have news."

Her breath caught. "Good or bad?"

"Good. I'm staying in Cherish a while longer. I told the owner of the chain I needed more days to scope out this area. Tom checked the registry and there's a room available for me for at least another week."

Julian had prolonged his stay because of her. He didn't say it. He didn't have to.

"Best of all, I can spend more hours with you, Nora." He bent his head and claimed her lips.

Her heart filled with three realizations as she weaved her fingers around his neck and kissed him back.

First, he was a man who liked kissing.

Second, they were definitely clicking.

And third, she wanted the kiss to never end.

CHAPTER 6

*O*n Monday morning, Nora reported to the lobby at eight a.m, blinking at the glittering sunlight streaming through the front window. The day promised a brightness that filled her to the core, though she suspected her optimism was based on something more than the weather.

Julian was still in Cherish. Therefore, she was sure to see him.

Today she'd chosen to wear a watercolor-print midi dress and leopard flats, and had snagged her rebellious hair into a semblance of a ponytail.

Samantha had begged to sleep in, promising to appear downstairs by ten. Her pre-lunch job required washing, drying, and folding laundry linens. Her afternoon chores necessitated waitressing in the dining room.

Humming, Nora stepped into Tom's office and scanned the pile of correspondence. The effort involved in running an inn of this size, of any size, never ceased.

She pushed a dusty ceramic rooster to the side of the

desk. What was it with Tom and roosters? And who was in charge of dusting? Surely they needed more than microfiber cloths. She glanced at the heavy draperies. They certainly needed a good whack with a towel.

Of course, a greater concern reared, having nothing to do with roosters or drapes.

Nora had come to the realization she'd never be able to help Tom in all the areas of innkeeping as she'd originally intended. There was simply too much to do. Outwardly, things ran efficiently. Behind the scenes proved the opposite.

In the days she'd been there, the air-conditioning and heating system had broken down with frightening regularity, and pricing and bookings constantly fluctuated.

Tom had surprised her by requesting that she examine the budget. He'd voiced concern because the numbers didn't add up, though he'd embroidered his statement with a crusty, "Being you're an accountant and all, you might see some extra money left over for repairs."

Her level of expertise was business foundations, she'd explained.

"Good," he'd muttered. "I think."

Nevertheless, he had confided in her, and she'd do her utmost not to let him down.

Seating herself at the desk, she struggled to concentrate on the ledgers. Soon her traitorous mind strayed to a more delightful thought:

Julian.

Julian and their Friday night date. She relived his kisses, their amiable bantering, and the desire in his molten-gray eyes whenever he gazed at her.

With a happy sigh of remembrance, she thrust the ledgers aside, leaned back in her chair, and rested her hands behind her head.

Once Friday evening had been behind them, she hadn't expected to see much of him again. His team members were still in town, and several closed-door meetings had ensued.

When he'd ducked out of a meeting on Saturday morning to spend a few minutes with her, he'd expounded on how he and his team evaluated costs, secured the best locations, applied for the required licenses, and the hours of ground-work all these assessments entailed. He kept appearing all day, finding her in Tom's office, the parlor, the dining room. He forever seemed to know where she was working.

He'd also invited her and Samantha to accompany him to church services on Sunday morning.

"I don't know anyone," he'd explained to Nora. "I'd like you to go with me."

She hung her hands on her hips. "Already, you are friends with more people in town than anyone. Soon, you'll be running for mayor."

He grinned. "If you recall, we were invited to church by the sheriff and his wife."

How could she forget?

In the end, Nora pleaded fatigue, Samantha seemed relieved, and Julian attended the service alone.

A brief knock on the office door yanked her back to the present.

"C'mon in," she called out.

Julian entered carrying a bouquet of pink-petaled daisies, bringing with him the whiff of clean air that was a part of him. He'd rolled up the sleeves of his denim shirt, exposing his muscled arms.

He leaned against the doorframe. "Good morning, gorgeous."

"Hi." She stood. "You've grown taller."

"Must be the flowers." He beamed and crossed the room

to hand her the bouquet—precious and heartening to lift her spirit. "These are for you. Daisies signify happiness, new beginnings, and loyalty."

"Thank you. They're beautiful." She set the flowers on the desk. "I'll go find a vase."

He caught her hand as she rounded the desk. "Flowers can survive for a few minutes without water."

"Is that a fact?"

He pressed a tender kiss to her forehead. "Absolutely."

She sought to maintain a cool, professional demeanor. However, how could she when he was so thoughtful and utterly masculine? *A heady combination.*

"Are your team members gone?" she asked.

"They left late last night for Atlanta. I'm still here, though."

She gazed up at his handsome face. "I see that."

"Aren't you curious about yesterday's church service?"

She shifted. "A little."

He ignored her lack of enthusiasm. "The sermon was inspirational and the worship music divine."

His soft reply made her feel ill-natured and impolite.

"Did you recognize every single person in the congregation?" she asked.

"Well, Max was there, for one."

"The June Bug singer? He and his wife are the puppy owners, right?"

"The very same."

He pulled a ladder-back chair over to the desk and told her to go ahead and sit again. He sat so near their knees touched, and the warmth of his body permeated her clothes.

"The puppy's name is Tiny Tim," she said.

He grimaced. "Right."

"Cute name. Tiny Tim reminds me of a Christmas story."

"True."

"I take it you don't like dogs?"

"I like dogs." He tapped his knuckles to his lips. "I'm just not a fan of small dogs."

"Your phobia?"

"Indeed."

"You mentioned you might tell me about it."

"Did I?"

"Yes, and I'm listening if you're ready to share."

He was unusually hesitant. His eyes reminded her of the color of the sky before a rainstorm.

"You must've had a frightening experience with a dog," she began.

Julian dismissed her statement in an offhand manner she didn't believe for a minute. The upcoming conversation was undoubtedly heavy on his mind.

"Have you heard the term *cynophobia?*" He seemed to have trouble finding his voice.

"Never."

"The definition is a person who is afraid of dogs. My fear persists no matter how hard I try to get over it. I realize it's totally irrational." He seemed annoyed with himself and expelled a breath.

"What prompted your fear?"

"When I was young, I petted a puppy who was chained to a fence outside by his owner." He rubbed his forehead. "I felt sorry for the sweet little dog. The day was hot, and he unexpectedly nipped me."

She winced. "How old were you?"

"Six."

"Were you hurt?"

"No, just frightened. Nonetheless, the memory and resulting panic stayed with me."

"Both children and dogs are inherently curious," she

assured. "The owner was irresponsible and raising an unsafe dog."

"I should be well over it." Julian pumped a foot, restless. "Thank you for listening."

Alrighty then. He'd obviously decided to end the conversation.

"Thank you for trusting me," she replied. Their gazes held, and the frozen band around her heart began to thaw. Behind his potent maleness, he was vulnerable, yet he'd chosen to reveal his emotions and had freely expressed his fears.

She realized vulnerability was the course to deeper human relationships, and he was reaching out to her. He didn't ask for pity. If anything, he acknowledged his worries.

"I'll help you sort it all out," she offered. "Your feelings, your reservations."

"I understand my fear on a cognitive level, though I can't seem to overcome it."

She managed a grin of assurance. "We'll take puppy steps."

"Puppy steps." He smiled, leaned over, and cradled her in his arms. She admired his earnestness, his honesty, and felt valued and cherished for being important enough to him to confess his helpless emotions.

The door was open, and she didn't care how many people saw them.

Tom, Louise, the staff, the guests. She didn't care, because there it was again, the invisible tug drawing her ever nearer to Julian.

No. Wait. He traveled the country, never staying in any area for long.

She pulled out of his arms and sprang to her feet. She fiddled with the daisy petals, a way of busyness to cover her rebellious emotions.

He cleared his throat and stood. "Like I said, the sermon was outstanding."

Right. The church service.

She realized he was watching her. "Oh," she replied.

"Oh?"

"How should I respond?"

"By agreeing to attend services with me this upcoming Sunday." He'd wiped his face clean of weakness. He'd found his way back to his competent self.

"You'll still be in town?" she asked.

"Will you?"

She laughed. "You know I will."

"Then so will I."

The tenderness of his assurance sent a tremor through her body.

"Marge Addyson, the associate pastor, is presenting a series on learning how to trust God's loving guidance," Julian continued. "Yesterday's sermon touched on being in a state of grace. Next Sunday she'll address how God speaks through unbelief."

"Sounds like her sermon was written just for me," Nora replied.

"God's truth communicates to us all, Nora. I suspect I need the pastor's sermon more than you." He shook his head.

He was too hard on himself, she thought.

"I haven't stepped a foot into a church since my divorce."

"Ryan Edwards will be singing *The Lord's Prayer*."

"The opera singer?"

"He'll be in town."

She narrowed her gaze. "Are you trying to bribe me with an opera singer?"

"Maybe."

She worked her bottom lip. "I told you my father loved

opera. He once said that an opera singer is classically trained to focus on diction and tonality."

"I'm aware."

"You don't like opera, but you know this about opera singers?"

"I know now."

Nora hesitated, noting Julian's wide grin. "Let me think about it. Samantha hasn't entered a church in ages, either."

"There's no time like the present."

"She hasn't indicated any interest."

With a gleam of amusement in his eyes, Julian said, "Encourage her by sharing two words."

"Opera singer?"

"Nope."

He was silent, evidently, waiting for Nora to ask again.

"Which are?" she relented, too inquisitive to stay mute.

"Joseph Slater."

"A name."

"A prominent musician," Julian corrected. "He's a Grammy-nominated recording artist recognized worldwide for his worship songs. He's singing at the Sunday service too."

"Samantha listens to bluesy jazz. She won't have any inkling who Joseph Slater is."

"Ask her." He brought her into his arms for a lengthy kiss. A while afterward, he ran a hand along her back and murmured, "I'm off to scout out an abandoned building near the railroad tracks that might be ideal for Fresh 'n' Good."

"You mean the old shoe shop that went out of business years ago? I remember shopping for shoes there."

"It's located in a timeworn mill, and there's plenty of foot traffic."

She grinned. "Shoe shop? Foot traffic? Clever."

"Right." He smiled. "My boss is pressuring me to come up with a suitable location for the restaurant … and soon."

She rested her head on his chest and drew a long breath. It felt so relaxing to be in his arms.

Remember? her rational brain intruded. Their time together was short-lived.

Unannounced, an inexplicable sadness settled over her.

Julian pulled back, studying her. He seemed aware of her change in mood and began regaling her with entertaining stories of various potential restaurant sites he'd encountered over the years—caves, train tunnels, and treehouses—and she couldn't help but laugh with him.

"I'll stop by the office later," he said. "Will you still be here?"

"Most likely."

"If you're not, I'll find you."

His answer prompted her wry response. "I'm sure you will."

"We'll go for dinner afterwards. My treat."

"You don't—"

"Sure I do. We'll celebrate."

"Why?"

"Because it's Monday."

"We're celebrating Monday?"

"Every day we're alive is a celebration."

She grinned. Julian, ever the optimist. "Where?"

"You're being picky when I'm treating?" He brushed his lips across her forehead. "Let's try Frank's Pizza. Tom recommended it as the best pizza place in town."

"From my recollection, it's the only pizza place within fifty miles."

"Another reason why I like it here. There are fewer choices." He chuckled at his own observation. "Please ask Samantha to join us."

"All right."

One more kiss, a gentle squeeze of his hand, and he was gone.

Nora stared at the empty doorway, then turned to the daisies on the desk. Daises were all about cheerfulness, fresh starts, and trustworthiness.

An accurate description of the flower. An accurate description of the man.

Julian's presence brought peace to her lonely, aching heart. His upbeat humor and romantic nature filled her with gladness.

However, he was busy with his work, and she was busy with hers.

Which was how her parent's marriage had evolved. Each had claimed their own set of chores and responsibilities. Theirs had been a business partnership rather than a love match.

A reality check of Nora's life emerged.

Perhaps that was the reason she'd been hesitant to find a man she could truly love after her divorce. Love had been elusive, and the youthful dreams of fairy-tale endings had indeed turned out to be make believe. She'd learned that hard lesson the hard way.

Through the years she'd lived alone, her dating life had been nonexistent. Often, she'd given herself pep talks to sign up for an online dating app, or attend social events on the weekend. All too often, she'd convinced herself that she had enough on her plate with the everyday challenges of raising a child.

She blew out a sigh and reexamined the inn's budget.

By midafternoon, her brain was ready to explode.

Tom was correct. The monthly income hardly covered expenses.

She flipped to another page on his budget sheet. The cost

of replacing burnt lightbulbs and broken hair dryers involved a revolving door of corrective upkeep. However, bigger problems emerged, beginning with preventive maintenance, which entailed comprehensive changes to the way things currently were handled

More capital was required and operating costs needed to be cut. If not, one guarantee for the Cherish Hill Inn loomed.

Bankruptcy.

CHAPTER 7

*N*ora was unable to accompany Julian to church the following Sunday, since Tom needed both her and Samantha to serve brunch. Samantha actually grumbled about not attending, and Nora suspected her discontent was because she wanted to see and hear Joseph Slater, the singer. However, Tom was looking wearier by the day and Nora wouldn't refuse him.

Julian didn't press Nora, and she was grateful for his quiet understanding.

"God will get tired of waiting for me," she declared with a half laugh.

"There's no wrong schedule for God," he said. "The best things from God aren't according to any agenda. He will move you when the timing is right. The highest blessings have no itinerary." As if to reassure her, he reached for her and held her close, and she appreciated his steadfastness and positivity.

Already she was beginning to know him—his faith, his strength, his convictions. Julian listened attentively, provided stability, and his optimism lifted her spirit.

Her conscience reminded she had fled from an intimate relationship with God because she believed she wasn't good enough.

Nothing had changed.

The old insecurity reared its head. Same misgiving, different seasons. She was a woman seeking faith, and looking to inspire her daughter to take the right path.

Trouble was, the world got in the way.

"You're always God's chosen child," Julian had counseled during one of their nightly text messaging sessions.

Her heart focused on finding a church. Her mind wasn't certain she was ready.

"Puppy steps," Julian had also advised, echoing her encouragement regarding his dog phobia. He'd included a smiley face emoji and wished her sweet dreams.

Yearning for a spiritual connection, Nora decided to attend the service on Wednesday evening. Clouds had given way to rain by late afternoon, and the constant drumming of droplets against the inn's windows had been soothing.

After dinner, she donned a bright-red raincoat over her black pencil skirt and printed silk blouse, snagged an umbrella, and marched the few blocks to the church for the seven o'clock service. June was heating up with the intensity of a Southern summer, and a rain-drenched breeze added a thickness to the air. Pansies and tree leaves drooped under the showers, and she splashed through the newly washed shimmer of water on the sidewalks. After church, this was a good night for warm cinnamon tea and cozy socks.

Julian had earmarked the evening to mentor Logan, a teenage boy enrolled in the Big Brothers Big Sisters program, and Samantha was waitressing. Nora hadn't told either of them of her resolution to attend church.

The previous week, Nora, Julian, and Samantha had

grabbed dinner at Frank's Pizza. Casually, Julian had opened his cellphone and introduced Samantha to Joseph Slater's worship songs. The guitar chords were simple, the melody basic, and Samantha was hooked. Julian remarked that Joseph had written the song, "Sing Glory Forever," which had been nominated for a Grammy award, slipping in the fact that Joseph and his wife, Scarlett, lived in Cherish.

"Louise mentioned that Scarlett volunteers at Canine Helpers." Nora glanced meaningfully at Julian while she spoke. "They train service dogs."

"Big dogs or little?" Julian inquired.

"Usually big."

"Piece of cake," he joked. "I like golden retrievers and German shepherds. Where do I sign up to help?"

"Service dogs come in all shapes and sizes," Nora clarified. "Small dogs are often used to warn their owners of changes."

He set down his pizza. "What kind of changes?"

"I'm not sure. Perhaps changes in their owner's mood? See for yourself."

His straight eyebrows drew together. "I'll consider it."

"Bravo." She raised her glass of iced tea and they clinked glasses.

Samantha, a slice of pepperoni pizza halfway to her mouth, paused to consider them, then ignored them in favor of the shaggy-haired teenage boy behind the counter.

As Nora entered Memorial Street Church, memories of past Sunday services rushed to the fore: the year she'd sat with her first grade class praying she wouldn't forget her memory verse, her dark-haired mother dabbing her eyes with a flowered handkerchief when the pastor's message was especially poignant, her tired-looking father wearing his Sunday finest—a navy suit, white shirt and tie.

Nora slid into a rear pew in case she felt compelled to dash out for some reason.

She didn't. In fact, she stayed until the final note of a long-forgotten hymn from her school days, "Amazing Grace," had been sung by the solo soprano.

How sweet the sounds, indeed, Nora reflected. Could it save someone like her?

She tapped her fingers to her heart, finished with a silent prayer, then lingered to sit with God for a while. "Praise you for the love you've given me and my daughter," she whispered. "I'm grateful. Please guide me on the right path."

She reminded herself the Lord sometimes took many days to reply. Often, He never replied at all.

No matter, for she was at a crossroads. The serenity of the peaceful church and the lyrical psalms had restored her balance on the heels of too many hectic days.

She rose, calmed and renewed, and fell into step with the other churchgoers. She exited the church and breathed in a lungful of clean air and wet earth. Post-rainstorm clouds streaked across the sky and a pastel sunset graced the heavens in strokes of gold and purple. The rain had stopped, and she slung her raincoat and handbag over her arm.

"Nora?" The recognizable, deep male voice made her pause. "I'm thrilled you're here."

Her mood soared as she turned to see Julian.

"Weren't you mentoring tonight?" she asked.

He took the stairs two at a time to reach her. "I did. Only Logan has a math test tomorrow and ducked out early to study. Are you headed back to the inn?"

"Where else?"

"Me too."

"What a coincidence."

He laughed and laced his fingers through hers. "We'll pass by Whitney's. Are you up for an ice cream cone?"

"I can't keep eating ice cream and pizza. Correction." She held up a hand. "I'd like to but—"

"Why not, then?"

"I want to continue fitting into the dresses I brought with me. I hoped to go down a size while I was here, rather than up one."

"Women are misguided. Stop reading fashion magazines and watching television and listen to real men." His gaze did a slow perusal of her figure, and he smiled. "A woman who fills out a skirt is sheer perfection."

Their stroll took them to the main street and the quaint shops that defined Cherish.

"There are pros and cons of living in a microscopic community," she observed.

"List the pros first."

"People will pitch in if there's a problem."

"You speak from experience?" he asked.

"My parents often needed assistance at the inn because of the ceaseless responsibilities."

He winked. "And here I assumed owning a successful inn meant sharing blueberry muffin recipes and collecting antiques."

She laughed, then sobered. "Once, a careless guest left a cigarette burning in his room. The fire was extensive and my parents were forced to close the inn for a month. The entire community donated money and furnishings and helped repair the damage. Then the whole town celebrated our reopening."

"God, family, and friends make all the difference." His gaze softened. "Let's list the cons."

"Let's?"

"I may be living here," he reminded her.

"A few months in Cherish is hardly a lifetime."

He shrugged. "Cons?"

"Towns this size can be small-minded and resistant to change. Residents are intent on safeguarding their routines and the manner in which they do business is paramount."

"Do you consider a Fresh 'n' Good restaurant an ostentatious eatery?"

"I never used the term *ostentatious*."

His lips tugged up at the corner. "Because *grandiose* is better."

"Fair warning, most folks here are content with plain and simple."

"There's nothing wrong with glamour. Studies prove that fine dining, an elevated ambiance, and superb service are highlights for diners."

She couldn't refute his rationale and kept silent.

They stopped in front of Whitney's. He stared at the sign listing the flavors as if he was searching for spelling mistakes. "A cone?" he suggested again.

Reluctantly, she shook her head, and they resumed their walk. "By the way, did you approve of the empty building near the train station?" she asked.

"I did, actually." He kept his fingers linked with hers. "Look, instead of discussing business, I'm interested in your thoughts on tonight's service."

"Marge Addyson is an inspirational pastor, and the worship music was beautiful. I recognized the hymns and sang all the lyrics. It's funny how certain memories never leave you."

"We're not navigating life alone," he said, rephrasing Marge's sermon. "God is always with us."

When they reached the inn, he paused. They stood beside a fence, shaded from view beneath a giant oak tree.

In a voice as rich as velvet, he said, "Thank you for another delightful evening."

His tender expression caused her insides to quiver, while a warning screamed in her ears. Proceed with caution. He's leaving. Why sacrifice your heart for a few hours of happiness?

She ignored the warning as his hands glided to her shoulders. He pressed her near and claimed her lips in a sweet, hungry kiss.

A few minutes later, they entered the lobby hand in hand. The clock in the hall chimed nine o'clock, and the restaurant had emptied out. Tom and Louise were nowhere to be seen.

Samantha erupted from the parlor, guitar in hand.

"Hi Mom." She smiled. "Hi Mr. Wilson." She frowned.

"Hi honey," Nora said while Julian extended a cordial hello.

"Guess what? Edison is driving to Cherish next weekend so we can rehearse. That is, if it's okay with you."

"Back up a minute." Nora briefly closed her eyes. "Rehearse for what?"

"His band. When we get back home to Virginia, he wants me to be a member."

"We're not leaving Cherish until the end of June."

"The weeks go by fast, Mom."

Truer words had never been spoken.

Nora glanced at Julian. The expression of disappointment on his face mirrored her own.

Why? They hadn't arranged to see each other once July appeared on the calendar. They were both merely passing through Cherish.

Nevertheless, she thought he might give her hand a slight squeeze, assuring her their relationship would continue.

He didn't.

His phone buzzed. He retrieved it from his pocket and glanced at the caller ID.

"Sorry." He excused himself. "One of the owners of Fresh 'n' Good is calling."

CHAPTER 8

$\mathcal{L}$ater the following afternoon, Julian and Fred Johnson, the Realtor representing Fresh 'n' Good, met to review the purchasing of the shoe shop building. Fred looked to be in his fifties, wasn't much taller than Samantha, and assured Julian he'd do whatever necessary to ensure an effective transaction. He was a long-time resident of Cherish and proudly elaborated on the town's history to whoever would listen.

Julian had recommended that Fresh 'n' Good purchase the building because the location was highly visible and, in his opinion, a hidden gem. The bustle of pedestrians and ample street parking were all advantages. He'd checked the interior of the shop, thickly coated in dust, and discovered racks and racks of shoes. Many were in their original boxes and perfectly preserved.

An inspection of the second and third floors exposed broken glass and vine-covered walls. The men's footsteps echoed on thick pine floors and splintered doors revealed worn paint and an upper room taken over by a flock of pigeons.

"Are the owners renovating everything?" Fred asked.

Julian grinned. "The use of a little elbow grease will convert the upper floors into condos."

After the meeting concluded, they stepped outside.

Clouds skittered across a cobalt sky. Summer had come to the Carolinas, and birdsong warbled from the trees. The breeze carried the candied fragrance of flowering magnolias.

Fred walked to his car and Julian followed.

"One more thing, Fred," he said.

"You want a pair of shoes from the 1970s?" Fred joked. "Help yourself. Many are still in style, and just need some sprucing up and leather polish."

"I'm set, thanks," Julian replied with a quick smile. "However, I'm thinking I want a permanent place to live here in Cherish."

"Permanent?" Fred made an impressive show of trying to keep his features noncommittal. "When we first spoke, you mentioned if the deal was successful, you planned to live in Cherish for six months, tops."

In the brief time Julian had known Fred, he seemed the type who followed his observations with a half-dozen questions. He didn't disappoint.

"Are you planning to rent out your house if you travel?" Fred inquired.

"No," Julian replied.

"Are you aware a town this size can have plenty of loudly expressed opinions, both good and bad?"

"Yes."

"The church is an integral part of many of the residents' lives."

"God comes first in my life too," Julian responded. "A home of my own has become important to me.

"To buy or to rent?"

94

"Either." Julian summarized his choice under Fred's shrewd gaze. "Whichever is quicker."

Fred's mouth curved in amusement. "The pretty Nora and her daughter are in town."

"I'm well aware."

"Tom bought the inn from Nora's parents many years ago," Fred continued. "They were in tough financial straits, and she was long gone by then."

"Where did she go?"

"Rumor was she eloped with her boyfriend. Some skinny kid from a nearby city who never kept a job."

Julian leaned against a tree. He allowed Fred all the time in the world to offer more details.

"Hmm." Fred's forehead creased. "You and Nora have been seen together on several occasions. In fact, you're the talk of the town."

The rumor mill again. Julian smiled.

"I'll look through the real estate listings and contact you."

As Fred headed for his car, people passing by exchanged friendly good wishes both to him and Julian.

Julian loved the fellowship of this old-fashioned town where children skipped exuberantly, and purple and pink petunias burst forth from decorative window boxes.

The idea of a place of his own opened a floodgate of emotions he'd kept bolted for many years. He'd spent the last several years of his life traveling across the United States, managing restaurants. There hadn't been much sense in purchasing a home he'd live in less than half a month.

Now, he intended to finally settle down. Not for six months. Permanently, although he hadn't figured out how to carry out his decision.

He took a seat on a bench, loosened his tie, and shrugged off his jacket.

It was time to settle down with a wife. A woman like

Nora—with wild black tangled hair, a striking contrast to her creamy complexion, high cheekbones, and amiable demeanor.

Her vivacious smile and quick wit drew him in. She was an intelligent beauty with a tall frame, small waist, and undeniable curves. The first time he'd kissed her, her long dark lashes had fluttered as she'd gazed up at him, and his world had come to a stop.

This was the woman, he'd thought. This was the woman who could change everything.

Undeniably, it would be difficult to start a relationship with someone who lived elsewhere.

So, why couldn't he ignore his attraction to her?

He rose, slung his jacket over his shoulder, and proceeded to the inn. As he passed Whitney's, he scanned the sign for the flavor of the day.

Dutch chocolate. Nora's favorite.

He paused and texted her. *Where are you?* he inquired.

Hawaii, came her reply. *I needed a break.*

He grinned. *Take a return boat to Cherish and meet me at Whitney's.*

I'm preparing a budget report for Tom.

Run it later.

I can't.

I have two words for you.

He visualized Nora's beautiful face, her forehead puckered in a frown.

Are you using the opera singer bait again?

Nope. He grinned, knowing any protest would soon die on her lips. Then he typed in the magical two words.

Dutch chocolate.

I'll be right there, came her quick reply.

Fifteen minutes later, Nora and Samantha headed toward him. Nora wore a lush floral sundress and sandals, and

Samantha had dressed in her pink beanie, jeans, and a balloon sleeve top. Samantha also lugged her guitar case, and her jaw tightened when she sighted him. Their quickening pace matched the quickening of his heart as his gaze refocused on Nora.

She tugged at a snarl in her hair as she and Samantha approached.

"Hi, Nora." He debated brushing a kiss on her cheeks, but opted for placing a hand on the small of her back. An innocent acknowledgment in front of her eagle-eyed daughter.

"Hi, Julian." Nora smiled a greeting.

"Greetings, Samantha," he went on. "Why the guitar?"

"Hello, Mr. Wilson." Samantha focused on his fingers, casually touching her mother. "I tagged along because I have a lesson at Musically Yours."

"With who?" He feigned surprise, although he'd arranged for Joseph Slater to teach her.

"*The* Mr. Joseph Slater."

"Those online lessons weren't cutting it?" Julian asked.

"Not so much."

"We'll walk you there. Then I'll buy you a takeout container of your favorite flavor."

"No thanks. I'm good." He didn't miss the grimace Samantha sent him.

Once they arrived at Musically Yours, Joseph Slater, a tall man with dark wavy hair and piercing blue eyes, hailed them.

Samantha was evidently starstruck, eyes glazed and totally speechless.

"If you care to meet my wife, she's over at Canine Helpers right now," Joseph said to Nora and Julian. "The center isn't far, and I'm sure she'd be delighted if you stopped by. I'll text her."

"Are there dogs there?" Julian's voice raised as he stepped back.

Joseph sent him a silent and quizzical, *You've got to be kidding.* Aloud, he answered, "I'm thinking yes. To begin with, Max dropped off Tiny Tim."

"The little dog?"

"Tiny Tim is a toy poodle and Yorkshire terrier mix," Joseph clarified.

"A Yorkipoo," Nora put in.

"A little dog," Julian repeated.

"We'll visit Canine Helpers." Nora said. "Thanks."

"Puppy steps," she reminded, as she half-dragged Julian and his stiff legs to Canine Helpers.

"A little dog," he reiterated. The wind caught his hair, and he wiped tiny beads of sweat from his forehead.

Scarlett Slater met them at the doorway. Her flamboyant red hair, deep green eyes, and jovial laugh should have put Julian at ease.

Nope.

He froze, rooted near the door, his gaze fixed on the fluffy miniature dog Scarlett held.

"Meet Max and Sarah's dog," she said. "Want to hold him?"

Nora loosened her grip on Julian's arm and cradled the dog. She and the dog shared a mutual, adoring gaze.

"Tiny Tim is friendly," Scarlett was saying. "We aren't training him. I'm watching him while Max and Sarah are working. He's a curious cutie."

Nora stroked his fur, murmuring, "You're also a sweetie." She swiveled to Julian. "Your turn?"

Aware of the women's gazes, he held his arms out straight, and Nora placed Tiny Tim in them. Scarlett politely remarked that Julian looked like he was holding a grenade rather than a dog weighing under ten pounds.

His face heated. At thirty-five years old, he shouldn't have to deal with such a fear. It was absurd. Determined, he peeked at Tiny Tim, then at the sky, pleading with God to deliver courage. When Julian looked back down, the dog's shiny black eyes were staring up at him affectionately.

"He's fond of you," Nora encouraged, depositing the dog back with Scarlett.

As they walked away, Nora found his fingers. "You were wonderful, Julian."

"I held Tiny Tim for all of ten seconds." His voice held a broad dose of uncertainty. "Surprisingly, though, it wasn't so bad."

His biggest lie ever. He'd almost neglected to breathe.

"Briefly is a promising start." Nora's response was soothing and nonjudgmental.

They sauntered past the park, leaving Canine Helpers far behind. He and Nora had analyzed his irrational fear, so rehashing it wasn't something he wanted to do. That settled, he reminded her they were going right past Whitney's.

"I can't resist." She patted her waistline. "I'll start my diet tomorrow."

"Breaking news," he said.

"Are you finally acknowledging I should lose weight?"

"I'm saying the opposite. You're perfect and don't get me started on your weight obsession." He kept her hand in his. "Before I forget, Fresh 'n' Good is slated to open by September or October."

"That's quick, considering how large the abandoned building is."

"They'll renovate a floor at a time." He gave her a wide smile. "What's your shoe size?"

"Huh?" She blinked. "My shoe size? Are you serious?"

"Always."

"Size eight."

"And Samantha's?"

"We wear the same size." She squinted at him. "Why?"

"Merely asking."

"Don't tell me you have a shoe fetish."

"I won't."

She sighed and airily dismissed his comment. "I think I've developed brain fog from analyzing Tom's budget. Or, more concisely, his lack of a budget."

"Did you find anything serious?"

"He's heading down a losing road, just like my parents."

"Is that why you're here? Because of your parents?"

"I should've been here for them when times got tough. I wasn't. Helping Tom is the least I can do."

"Guilty conscience?" he inquired.

"Always." She pushed out a breath and waved away the question. "I'll prepare another report for Tom, though my gut instinct is he'll suffer a substantial income loss after your restaurant opens."

"Disclaimer. Fresh 'n' Good isn't mine." Julian clipped a hand through his hair. "I'm merely the manager."

"Spouting that fact doesn't make you blameless, Julian."

In his opinion it did. Just like Nora shouldn't blame herself for not being there for her parents. He told her as much.

"Let's look at the bright side." He gestured toward Whitney's. "An established chain will attract more visitors, and the additional revenue is a win-win."

"We won't know for sure, and I won't be here." Her gaze volleyed to the wooden planters bedecked with purple pansies beneath Cherish Styles and Clips. "My boss is already asking if it's necessary that I'm gone until early July."

"Everyone is expendable, Nora."

"Thanks for the vote of confidence. When someone is no longer of value, I assume you mean they can be discarded?"

"I didn't mean anything like that."

"Like what? Like you're a control freak, telling me when and where I can and cannot work? Who is important and who is not?"

"You must realize my beliefs by now." He sucked in a sharp breath. "What brought this on?"

In his mind, he answered his own question. Frustration. The same frustration he felt at the realization they would soon be parted.

As they neared the ice cream shop, Nora fixed her gaze on the Whitney's sign. Julian was watching her, so a tree root growing up from the sidewalk caught him off-guard. He tripped and lost his balance. Nora tripped with him, and his arm shot out to prevent her fall. Her ankle bent, awkwardly contorting.

"Ouch!" Her voice held surprise. Her expressive eyes held pain.

Worry, quick and consuming, surged through him. "Are you hurt?"

"I'm okay." She offered a wobbly, reassuring smile. He extended his arm, and she seized it in a death grip. "I think I twisted my ankle."

He supported her the last few feet.

Limp. Limp. Limp.

He steadied her, eased the unruly hair from her forehead, and pulled out a chair in front of Whitney's. Gratefully, she sank down.

He loosened her sandal and ran a hand over her bare ankle. Nothing appeared broken, and he exhaled a relieved breath.

"Rest here." He yanked out his phone. He'd done a fairly competent job maintaining his composure, though his heartbeat hadn't yet returned to normal. "I'll call a cab to drive us."

"Don't be ridiculous, Julian. I can hobble a few blocks."

"Nora—"

"I insist."

"Can you move your ankle?"

She flexed her foot and grimaced. "Yes."

"I'll contact Joseph Slater." Julian fired off a rapid text. "He'll tell Samantha to meet us back at the inn when her lesson is finished."

"Sure."

A waitress appeared. "May I take your order?"

Nora massaged her ankle. "Believe it or not, Dutch chocolate ice cream isn't in my immediate plans anymore."

"We'll take a rain check. Thanks." Julian draped his arm around Nora's shoulders. "If you insist, we'll walk slowly."

She leaned against him all the way back to the inn, which delighted Julian.

Samantha didn't share his enthusiasm when she dashed through the front door.

"I'll find Louise," she volunteered. "She's competent."

Her message to Julian was crystal-clear: We don't need you. Women take care of each other.

Of late, Samantha had spent her off hours with Louise. She'd shown Louise several chords on the guitar, and Louise had taught Samantha how to knit her own beanies. Despite the age difference, both the older woman and the teen seemed to crave the companionship and someone to listen to them.

"Elder hunger," Nora had half joked, when he'd reported his observation.

"They're bonding," he acknowledged. "And Samantha has taken to calling Louise *Auntie*."

"Samantha never knew her grandparents, and I'm reminding myself not to interfere, because then their dynamics will be different," Nora said. "Louise is an admirable and wise influence. Even Tom is warming up to Samantha."

"You're a smart woman and caring parent, Nora," Julian responded. "They're teaching each other to observe the world through each other's perspective."

Nonetheless, Samantha was still possessive of Nora when it came to Julian.

In many ways, she reminded him of himself with his own mother. She'd been a single parent, and as the oldest son, he was protective of her.

He ordered himself to be understanding and validate Samantha's feelings, then closed his eyes and whispered a plea to God for guidance.

a sprained ankle, Nora soon learned from Louise, demanded four treatments: rest, ice, compression, and elevation.

"RICE," Louise declared. "An easy acronym to remember."

The tenderness and swelling had subsided. Even so, Louise insisted Nora not place any undue stress on her ankle.

Julian heartily approved.

From Louise's sidelong grin, Nora suspected she was relieved Nora wouldn't be waitressing.

"For how long?" Nora asked.

"Three days, possibly less," the doctor advised when Julian had brought her into his office for an examination. "Your ankle seems stable. The pain and stiffness you've described is moderate, and there are no torn ligaments."

And so she rested.

The following day, an early morning dawn cast a rosy hue across the sky, and Nora flopped in a rocker on the porch. Samantha and Louise checked out guests at the front desk, and Julian was on a phone consultation with one of the owners from Fresh 'n' Good.

Nora had nearly closed her eyes when Tom greeted her with a gruff, "Are you awake?"

Her eyes flew open. "I dozed for a second. The air is pleasant and peaceful and—"

"Mind if I join you?"

She swept out her hand. "This is your inn."

Tom collapsed next to her with a grunt. Silently, they rocked back and forth for several beats.

"I remember these same swaying tree branches and summer breezes," she said. "As I grew older, there were many occasions when I would've traded my eyeteeth to hang out with friends and swim at the community pool." She sighed, half to herself. "Alas, those dreams weren't meant to be because of the constant work schedule."

Tom stopped rocking and fixed her with a blunt stare. "May I be frank?"

"Absolutely."

"By the time your parents sold me the inn, I suspected their hearts were no longer in it."

Nora's eyes widened in surprise. "The inn was the center of their universe."

"No, you were, from what I understand," he said. "Perhaps the reason their passion died was because they lost you."

"They didn't 'lose' me. We just … lost touch." Or rather, she broke ties with them. Angry and rebellious, she'd rashly eloped with her boyfriend and moved far away from Cherish to prove she was adult enough to make her own choices. Good or bad. Right or wrong.

"Are you returning to your accounting job soon?" Tom's voice interrupted her thoughts, her misgivings.

"My boss texts every day. Apparently, the firm is finally beginning to appreciate me."

"Huh."

Huh?

She pushed the rocker hard with her toe. "Why bring this up?"

"Maybe you should consider a change of career."

She steeled herself. Tom was parroting Julian's words. Next he would offer a "Nobody is expendable" speech.

"To do what?" She pressed her hands together in her lap.

"You have a knack for innkeeping." His gaze swept the lawn, and the overgrown bushes begging for a pruning. "I'm thinking about eventually slowing down and retiring. Louise has dropped hints and I'm looking for someone competent to take over."

Someone like her?

A myriad of reasons to say no came to the fore. She'd disconnected from the inn years ago. Sure, she'd returned, but only for a short time.

"Are you suggesting me?" she asked.

"It crossed my mind."

She gazed at him. "I prefer a reliable and steady income."

He remained silent for so long, she wondered if he had heard her. She was about to voice more opinions when he said, "Spoken as a responsible and careful accountant."

"From our shared experiences, you can't refute that owning an inn is a 24/7 job with no holidays." She shook a disobedient curl from her face. "A substantial cash reserve is essential to weather the losses. Most inns operate at only 50 percent capacity, not to mention the extra capital required for health and property insurance. I won't live on hope, Tom. Teenagers are expensive, plus there's college for Samantha in a few years."

"At my advanced age, I've learned nothing is 100 percent secure. For example, take your twisted ankle, or my heart attack, or the new restaurant." His lined face sagged heavily with regret. "Our days on Earth are brief and constantly changing."

*O*n Sunday, neither Nora nor Samantha waitressed, and Julian volunteered to walk them to church for the service. The doctor had proclaimed Nora's ankle healed, due to the proper rest and the ice she'd frequently applied.

The previous evening at an impromptu dinner, Julian had mentioned to Samantha that Joseph Slater would be playing guitar at the service. As he no doubt anticipated, she nearly popped out of her pink canvas sneakers at the opportunity to attend church.

"You're incorrigible," Nora had murmured to him.

He widened his eyes. "Me?"

"You have a talent with words. Two words in particular."

"Joseph Slater?"

"Um, no."

His earnest gaze fastened on her. "You're beautiful."

She felt her cheeks pinken as he grabbed her hand under the table, his thumb caressing her palm while Samantha dug into her strawberry shortcake.

*"R*eady?" he asked when they met in the lobby. Then he did something Nora never expected. He ignored her and chatted the entire few blocks to church with Samantha about Joseph Slater's music.

After the inspiring service, Nora, Samantha and Julian stood outside and conversed with numerous townspeople they'd come to know.

"Are you both interested in a sneak peek at the vacant

building Fresh 'n' Good bought?" Julian gave Nora a gallant bow. "However, only if you feel up to the walk."

"I'm fine," Nora said.

Samantha declined. "I'm going back to my room to practice guitar. Mr. Slater said he'll email me the music for his worship song, and I can't wait to play the chords for Auntie Louise and Uncle Tom."

Nora and Julian exchanged knowing, smiling glances.

"How about we bring you a slice of Frank's pizza when your mother and I return?" Julian asked Samantha.

"Jake is bringing a pepperoni pizza to the inn." Samantha signaled to a shaggy-haired youth standing a few feet away. "We're eating lunch together."

Nora looked from Jake to her daughter. "What happened to Edison?"

"Old news, Mom. Jake saw me in church just now and texted about grabbing a pizza. I texted him back and said sure."

"I didn't see you texting."

"Teenagers text quick. We don't even look at our phones."

Nora squinted at the tall, lanky boy. "How old is he?"

"He's my age."

"Where did Jake get your cellphone number?"

"Auntie Louise."

Nora's lips pursed. "She gave him your number?"

"She's friends with his parents." Samantha smiled. "Everyone is friends with everyone here."

"You make it sound like a reason to stay."

"This town is awesome."

When had Samantha experienced such an abrupt change of heart? The interest of a caring community had had a positive influence, and that realization brought a grateful smile to Nora's face.

Along the way to the vacant building, Nora and Julian

peered through the sparkling-clean windows of boutique stores, discussing the unique giftware—mason jars, herbal gardens, flowered tea towels, and vintage postcards. Laughing and conversing with him had taken on an otherworldly quality all its own.

"God's grace is upon us." Julian said, bringing up the sermon. "He is our strength."

"No matter what adversities come onto our path." Nora repeated the pastor's declaration. "Leave the negative behind."

"Imagine the tiny mustard seed. Faith grows sure and steady in our lives."

"And you are planting the seeds."

"God is also, as well as your parents. They took you to church all those years ago. Don't skip that part because the process of faith doesn't happen overnight."

When they reached the building, Julian extracted a key and led her inside.

He pointed to the racks of shoes. "I convinced the owners to distribute these to Big Brothers Big Sisters, and then the rest to the community. However, I found a gift for you, Cinderella. Size eight, correct?" He dusted off a bench and beckoned her to sit, then reached behind the counter for a box.

An objection formed on her lips.

He kissed her, smothering her protest, then prompted her to open the box.

Inside was a tiny crystal slipper.

She held it up to the sunshine pouring through the window, admiring the shoe's rainbow reflection and design. "Julian, this is hardly a size eight."

"Size two is the best I could manage." He slipped her a rueful glance, then kissed her palm. "I don't recommend you wear such a high heel, especially with your recovering ankle.

When I began cleaning the store, this discovery was magical. I researched and learned the slipper was exhibited in the front display case."

She hid a smirk behind the slipper. "Only one?"

"There's more than one?"

His grin was so boyishly appealing that she laughed. "Don't you remember any fairy tales?"

"Hmm. I'll try to find a match." He seemed relaxed as he mangled the story lines of several fairy tales with charming wittiness. He obviously did know his fairy tales—probably better than she. Another quality she appreciated. His humbleness.

She blew him a kiss. "Thank you, Prince Charming. Thank you." Warmth radiated through her chest. This was happiness.

He smiled, his laugh lines evident. She hadn't noticed them before. "I was hoping for more than an air kiss."

"How about shoes in my size?" she teased.

He tugged out a box from a section labeled size eight and presented her with a pair of red Mary Jane shoes, flat, closed toe, and embellished with a strap. "Will these be okay?"

"They were popular in the 1900s."

"You'll wear them?"

"Certainly. They're back in style." She set the box beside her, then rubbed her thumb over the mirror-like glass of the slipper. "I'll treasure your gifts always—mementoes of my stint in Cherish."

"A month isn't nearly long enough." His voice deepened, a throaty murmur.

"A month is all we have." There, she'd said it aloud. The elephant in the room.

"Why? We have so much in common. Our shared humor, how well we get along." His gray eyes welled as he swept a kiss along her brows. His lips traveled, exploring her cheeks, lightly kissing her mouth.

She congratulated herself on doing a fabulous job of maintaining her poise. "Lots of folks share commonalities. My priority is my daughter and livelihood, and an unpaid four-week position in Cherish doesn't count."

He threw her a convincing grin. "Our priorities regarding family and friendships are the same. Our …"

Love.

He didn't say the word aloud. He didn't have to. She saw the emotion in his eyes, his smile. He was falling in love with her. And she was falling in love with him.

He stared at her, refusing to let go. The dusty shop, the glass slipper, the entire world melted into nothingness. All that mattered was Julian's intense, smoldering gaze.

No, no. Her hours in Cherish were earmarked for Tom, for the memory of her parents. She hadn't come searching for romance.

Though here it was. Or rather, here *he* was. Julian.

Moral and honorable, he truly cared about her and her daughter. A man she valued as a friend. A man she could happily spend a lifetime with.

He leaned close and cuddled her. His strong arms wrapped around her, and her soft body molded to his chest.

She ran a finger across his lips. "Julian, we both know this isn't a good idea. I'm leaving soon and so are you. We shouldn't complicate matters."

"I'm not leaving."

An odd feeling fluttered in her stomach. "You're not?"

"I'm setting down roots in Cherish." Before she could ask any questions, he kissed her again—tender and gentle and passionate, as was his nature. He took his time. The man who loved to kiss. "And I'm not ready for you to leave either," he murmured.

She rested her head on his chest, hearing the quiet thud of his heartbeat.

This was news. He was asking her to stay.

Wasn't he? Or was he demanding?

"Competent help is necessary for the business side of a restaurant," he continued. "The main office has its own accounting branch, though each eatery runs independently."

"All these job offers," she muttered. "From Tom and now you."

"I don't understand."

"Nothing. Nothing. Whom do you normally employ in these instances?"

"Usually locals," he replied.

"There's your answer."

"What was my question?"

"Aren't you offering me a job?"

"Perhaps, if you were a local."

She stiffened. "Which, as you undoubtedly know, I'm not."

"But you *were* once, and could become again."

Beats of silence. Awkward seconds while she debated how to respond.

"Are you asking me to remain in Cherish?" Her voice tripped over the question. She didn't wish to appear needy. A strong dose of embarrassment would surely pour through her if she'd misinterpreted his words.

"Your choice. Whatever your current salary is in Virginia, I'll match it if you relocate here and I'll add a yearly bonus along with sick leave and benefits."

She narrowed her gaze. "Once again, you're trying to tell me how to live my life."

"You already have two jobs between the Cherish Hills Inn and your full-time accounting position. I was musing aloud."

"Musing?" She grabbed hold of the shoes. "Sounds like you were doing more than musing."

"You jumped to a conclusion."

"Did I?"

He eyed the shoes. "Are you planning to throw those at me?"

"It crossed my mind."

"Forget it," he said.

Forget what? His offer or throwing the shoes at him?

They packed up. Their pace scarcely resembled their earlier stroll to church. Now, they didn't speak, their steps quick. She tucked the boxes under her arms, refusing his request to carry them for her. One held the Mary Jane shoes —sensible and practical. The other boasted the glass slipper —a fanciful dream.

She refused to chide herself for their disagreement. Yet later that evening she stared at her bedroom ceiling for hours. Their argument had stemmed largely from her being self-protective. No one could blame her for being anxious about getting too close to someone. Not if they knew her experience, relying on a teenage husband who'd bolted when nights with a newborn got rough.

Julian's offer, if indeed he'd made an offer, was too much, too unexpected. She was strong and independent. She'd established herself as a career woman and created a stable home in Virginia. She and Samantha were content.

Weren't they?

CHAPTER 10

*T*hree days later, Nora decided she was returning to Virginia and taking Samantha with her.

"We're leaving almost a week early?" Samantha displayed the calendar on her phone and put her finger on the date. "Why?"

"Aren't you glad?" Nora laid her folded chiffon dress and silky sea-green scarf in her suitcase. "You preferred not to be in Cherish, anyway."

"I changed my mind. I like everyone here." Samantha slung her hands on her slender hips. "Did you tell Uncle Tom and Auntie Louise?"

"Not yet, honey." Nora rubbed her upper arms, her muscles stiff.

She'd secure an internet setup between Tom's computer and hers because she didn't want to leave him hanging, and intended to work on his budget remotely. Through questioning the staff, she planned to implement cross-training as a means to save money. There was no reason why the woman who handled the laundry couldn't help out at the front desk during the busy hours, or the teenage busboy update Tom's social media on a regular basis. However, Nora was mindful the personnel shouldn't be overburdened, and resolved to share her concerns with Tom.

"I love my guitar lessons with Mr. Slater." Samantha darted her gaze to the guitar propped in the corner. "Besides, I've finally started to make friends. Jake gushed about the fantabulous music program. Music and math are his favorite subjects, exactly like me."

"We have so much in common," Julian had told Nora.

Memories of their afternoon in the shoe shop surged, and her throat clogged

Tears had filled his eyes as he'd swept a kiss along her brows, her cheekbones, before affectionately kissing her mouth. Her stomach had quivered at his gentle touch, so tender despite his compelling masculinity. Julian wasn't ashamed to show his emotions. As a little boy, he'd been taught not to cry, yet, as an adult man, he hadn't hidden his tears.

He'd texted her the previous evening. Then he'd left a voice message. He and his Realtor were viewing homes for sale in Cherish all day.

She never responded, nor did she disclose her resolution to leave. Soon, she told herself. Soon. Just not today, although she didn't know if she could endure living apart from him.

Now that she was in her thirties, she strove to be wiser in a relationship. Nonetheless, she wasn't prepared to sacrifice her heart solely to have it shattered. True love and fairy-tale romances? Not possible, at least not in her life.

Still, she prayed—even though God hadn't answered.

"Nice shoes, Mom." Samantha glared down at Nora's shoes. "Red matches well with our aprons tonight."

"I'm not waitressing anymore. There are other jobs to attend to."

"Another decision?"

"A necessary one."

"You're making too many choices without considering what I want." Samantha stomped from the bedroom, declaring she was heading to Frank's Pizza to share a calzone with Jake and then would report to the restaurant.

Nora sighed, closed her suitcase, and set it on the floor. She couldn't be a coward forever. She was obligated to inform Tom.

Tom first. Then Julian. The idea of leaving Julian brought a leaden hollowness to her chest. She sucked in a healthy whiff of resolve and, emboldened, marched down the stairs.

The angry voices emerging from Tom's office caused her to pause.

"I'm ready to retire, Tom." Louise's distinct Southern drawl held an edge. "We're at an age when we should think more about ourselves and less—"

"Cherish Hills Inn is an institution," Tom cut her off. "I've considered what you're saying regarding retirement."

"How long then?"

"A few months."

"Months?" Louise's voice raised. "I'm not a spring chicken anymore. I can't wait months."

"How about a few weeks?"

"No!"

Nora wasn't sure when Julian appeared beside her. He pushed open the office door to reveal Louise and Tom. They stood, hands clenched at their sides, confronting each other.

Louise's chin was high, her complexion reddened.

Tom made a sweeping motion with his arm. "Julian, can you talk some sense into this woman? I can't up and leave the inn tomorrow."

"Listen, you two lovebirds." Julian said, while Nora held her breath. "No decision needs to be finalized this evening. Tomorrow is soon enough to plan your retirements."

Louise's posture remained stiff. "I've never visited Arizona. I want to see the Grand Canyon."

"You will," Julian assured her.

"Come, my peach cake. I'll treat you to dinner." Tom bent to plant a kiss on her cheek and she swatted him away.

"You own this restaurant, you cheapskate," she blustered. "I better mean more to you than a discount date."

"I'll take you anywhere," he called as she fumed from his office.

She whirled. Her eyes sparked. "Arizona! Our next meal together will be eaten in Arizona."

"What's in Arizona?" Tom asked no one in particular when she slammed the door behind her.

"The Grand Canyon," Nora and Julian replied.

$\mathcal{T}$he next two hours dragged. Nora had requested Julian allow her space because crunching Tom's budget numbers awaited. He'd sighed resignedly, tipped his head with a reminder he'd text later, then retreated.

In frustrated silence, she sank into the desk chair.

She couldn't carry on a reasonable conversation with Julian after the scene with Tom and Louise. Abruptness wasn't part of her nature, and she'd been ill-mannered for dismissing him so shortly. Nevertheless, her duty to Tom was paramount, and costs should be cut to reduce his bottom line. Negotiating lower vendor rates was a sensible beginning, and she'd suggest Tom schedule in-person meetings with the sellers. Also, guests staying extra nights could reuse towels and request when they'd prefer their rooms cleaned, not necessarily every day, requiring no additional cost to the inn besides a simple note on the door. She grinned at the ceramic rooster, running a finger along its dusty feet. She'd find all the roosters a happy home at the thrift store.

When she was too tired to continue, she climbed the stairs to her room, dropped into the rocking chair, and removed her shoes. As she set the shoes in her lap, a knock sounded at the door.

"Nora?" a familiar male voice called.

She sat up. "Julian?"

"May I come in?"

His tone sounded oddly urgent, and she frowned. "Yes. The door is unlocked."

He quickly stepped inside. "I assume you haven't heard the news because you didn't respond to my texts."

His unintended accusation raised her hackles. "I left my phone in my room. I just returned and haven't checked for messages."

"I'm sorry. I didn't mean—" His appearance was ragged. He looked scruffy, a stubble of beard on his chin. She hadn't noticed it earlier.

"What is it?" Panic gripped her chest. She half stood. The shoes fell to the floor.

"Tom suffered another heart attack. He's in the intensive care unit."

"No." In apprehension and despair, she slumped back into the seat.

"Don't worry." Julian crossed the room to give her shoulder an encouraging squeeze. "His condition is stable."

She pushed herself up. "We need to go."

They leapt into motion.

Nerves battered Nora in the fleeting distance to the hospital. She drove her car, and they avoided the "What if anything happens to Tom?" topic. Quiet dominated the space between them. Where had their relaxed banter gone? The easy chatting she and Julian once shared?

Julian finally spoke, saying he'd texted Samantha. "She's with Jake and she wants us to phone her when we learn anything. Louise is already in the hospital and blaming herself since her and Tom's argument."

"Ridiculous," Nora murmured as she parked.

Soon after they arrived and had consoled Louise, Tom's condition was attributed to indigestion, and the doctor declared he would be released in the morning. Louise insisted on staying the night with him, and Nora phoned Samantha with the heartening message. In the hush of the late June evening, Nora and Julian walked back to her car.

Julian opened the door for her, then went around to the passenger side. These actions defined him forever the gentleman.

They sat together in the parking lot. The hour neared midnight, the lot uncrowded save for a few cars passing now and then.

"There's a subject I wish to discuss," Julian began without preamble.

She started, attempting not to act as interested as she was. "Such as?"

"I was thinking … hoping … that we can visit the church tomorrow and schedule an appointment with the pastor to begin preparations for our marriage."

Her breath hitched. Her skin tingled. "Us? Marry?"

"Yes. I love you. And I'm almost certain you love me."

"Almost certain?" Her voice sounded soft and halting to her ears.

He grinned. "I'm fairly certain. Right, okay, I *am* certain. I hope to adopt Samantha and already love her as my own."

"Samantha … I can take care of her. I've done that all my life."

"I'd like the opportunity to be a father to her. I know what you wish to provide her, and I want the same. A place where she is surrounded by people who care and support her. A town that prays and values church and God." He swallowed. "I made an offer on a brick ranch-style home. I'll put a hoop up over the garage for Samantha."

Nora tried to speak. Elated tears misted her vision. "She's never played basketball."

"Once we're married, I'll teach her how to shoot baskets. The house even has a yard."

"Big enough for a dog?"

"I'm not that brave."

"Wait. You're certain that I love you?"

"Beyond a doubt." His lips twitched. "You've voiced it many times without words. I see it in your eyes. I feel it whenever I kiss you."

Tears streamed down her cheeks, and he cradled her face in his hands. "Why are you crying?"

"An honest Christian community is the only place I want to live."

"Me too. I've asked myself, where are we in our lives, Nora? Where are we headed?" With a touch of his fingertips, he absorbed her tears.

She gazed at the handsome man sitting by her side, and her heart pitched.

They were headed in the same direction. Together. Wherever she traveled would always be in partnership with him.

"The house is located near the high school." He met her stare, his gaze intense, gauging her reaction. "The district is ranked number one in the state."

Nora couldn't contain her smile. "Samantha mentioned the school is top notch."

"And you … you could …"

"Please don't suggest running the inn. I'll help Tom, though it's not my dream job."

A million ideas floated through her head.

"Perhaps set up your own accounting business and handle the reports for the Cherish Hill Inn and Fresh 'n' Good."

"True." She didn't want the inn to fail and could work with Tom to keep it solvent.

Julian hugged her, then tipped up her chin. "Nora Lancaster, will you marry me?" His voice was solemn and husky.

She gazed into his pure gray eyes, and a rush of tenderness ran through her. Her husband to be. Thrilled, she nodded her agreement. "Yes. Yes. I'm in love with you, Julian Wilson."

He traced his fingers along her cheekbone. His woodsy male scent flooded her senses. "I knew it," he whispered.

He kissed her like a man who'd fallen head over heels in love.

Happiness filled her spirit. Soon, she and Samantha would carry his name.

Beneath the cotton of his polo shirt, his chest was comforting and solid. Her fingers covered his thumping heart.

He was silent for a long beat. "I fell in love with you the first night in the dining room, when you announced the chef was agreeable."

"He seems pleasant, as long as you don't cross him."

"Good to know."

"And you had me believing you were a vegetarian." She chuckled. "I get your sense of humor."

"Appreciated."

Looking back, she realized she had fallen in love with him at that same moment—when they'd mopped up spills, and spoke of cleaning kitchen counters, and discussed her and her daughter's similarities.

After decades of running away, Nora and Julian had arrived at a place, a home, where they truly belonged. A family to raise her daughter.

Surely, this was a day to remember, and a joyful home-coming to cherish.

EPILOGUE

*D*ear Auntie Louise and Uncle Tom,

How is Arizona? I can't believe it's been two years since you moved there. I loved the pictures of the Grand Canyon you sent. It's so cool, and I'm looking forward to vacationing with you there. Mom and Dad said you're living in an RV and traveling around the country.

I finished my senior year in high school and am counting the days until I attend college. I'm majoring in music and composing worship songs on the guitar. Mr. Slater said they're decent, but he always says nice things.

We attend church every week, and often on Wednesday nights too. Mrs. Addyson is one of my favorite preachers. Her sermons are awesome, and I believe she is speaking directly to me. How does she know? Mom said the sermons always resonate with her too and we discuss prayer a lot. Dad said prayer is a comfort and God will always be there for us.

Mom works at her accounting business during the day, and Dad said buying Cherish Hills Inn from Uncle Tom is the best decision he ever made after he left Fresh 'n' Good. I think adopting me was his best decision. When I told him, he agreed, then asked me to shoot hoops in the driveway. I'm getting fairly decent at basketball, though not as good as him.

It was awkward at first after he and Mom got married. I didn't know what to call him, but he was patient. I decided on Dad, because he is my Dad, and he seemed really happy when I told him.

He buys flowers for no reason. When I asked him why, he said it was to celebrate another day. He also gives Mom and me handwritten cards. His messages always make me smile, and Mom says he's a romantic at heart.

He also volunteers at Big Brothers Big Sisters every week, and I often go along to help. The little kids are so cute and always need assistance with their homework.

Fresh 'n' Good is a popular eatery, and Dad says they're healthy competition for the inn. We'll eat at both places when you come visit Cherish, and you can tell me your opinion. I like the inn's food better. The first thing Dad did when he bought the inn was to install a new coffee machine.

P.S. Did I tell you we got a dog? He's one of Molly Belle's puppies and adorable. Sheriff Nicholas reminded Dad that he'll get big. Dad looked kind of nervous, though Mom assured him small dogs are friendly and that she'd help him. I'm not sure what she was talking about. Then they kissed, as usual. So it's all good.

P.P.S. You asked about my boyfriend, Jake. He's old news. I met a cute boy at Whitney's Ice Cream shop. His name is Sebastian. I hope you get to meet him before I break up with him when I go to college.

Please write soon.

Love,

Samantha Wilson

· · ·

THE END

A NOTE FROM JOSIE

Dear Reader,

Thank you for reading *A Homecoming To Cherish.* I hope you loved my sweet inspirational romance. I've enjoyed creating the fictional, faith-filled community of Cherish, and hope you have come to love the characters as much as I loved writing them.

Sometimes a story and romance just clicks, and this happened when I wrote the heroine, Nora, and the hero, Julian. I found their sweet, inspirational romance irresistible.

I also had fun creating Samantha, Nora's teenage daughter.

Please help other people find *A Homecoming To Cherish* by posting your review.

A Homecoming To Cherish is available in ebook, paperback, Large Print Paperback, hardcover and Audiobook.

The final book in the series is A Summer To Cherish, featuring a despondent artist losing his vision, and the spunky, independent woman who encourages him.

I'd love to meet you in person someday, but in the meantime, all I can offer is a sincere and grateful thank you. Without your support, my books would not be possible.

As I write my next sweet or inspirational romance, remember this: Have you ever tried something you were afraid to try because it mattered so much to you? I did, when I started writing. Take the chance, and just do something you love.

My Spotify Play List for A Homecoming To Cherish is here.

With sincere appreciation,

Josie Riviera

Want more sweet sweet and clean "Cherish" romances?

Click here.

Or grab Cherished Hearts.

The entire series! 6 sweet, inspirational romances in 1 giant boxed set.

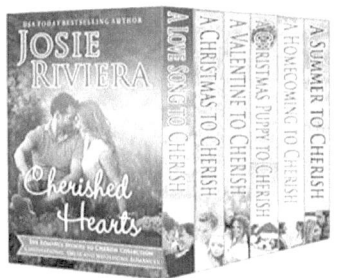

CRISSY'S CHICKEN 'N' DUMPLINGS RECIPE

Ingredients:

1 pound uncooked chicken breast chopped

5 cans low-sodium chicken broth

1 family-size can of cream of chicken soup

2 1/2 stalks of celery chopped

1/2 large bag of frozen super-sweet white corn

3 russet potatoes, peeled and diced

1/4 pound baby carrots, chopped

1/4 teaspoon onion powder

1/2 teaspoon black pepper

Fresh rosemary, if desired.

Dumplings:
    1 1/2 cups flour
    1 egg
    1/2 cup milk
    1/2 teaspoon salt
    1 1/2 teaspoons baking powder

Directions:

Place chicken broth, chicken, and potatoes in pot on medium-high heat and bring to a boil.

Cover and boil until chicken is tender, approximately 7-10 minutes, depending on size of chicken pieces.

Reduce heat to medium.

Add cream of chicken soup, seasonings, and remaining vegetables.

Keep covered and boil 15-20 minutes or until vegetables are tender.

For dumplings:

Add all the ingredients to a large bowl and mix to combine. Using your hands or a spoon scoop into dumplings, about the size of an overflowing tablespoon. The dough will be sticky.

Carefully drop dumplings into boiling soup or stew and cook for 15-20 minutes, or until dumplings no longer fall apart. Cover with a tight-fitting lid while cooking.

Enjoy!

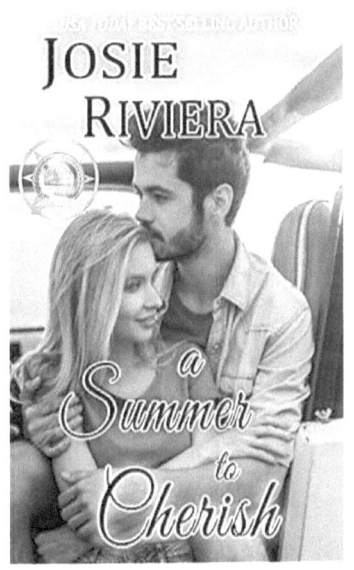

Chapter One

Every child is an artist. The problem is how to remain an artist once he grows up.

- Picasso

A famous artist didn't just disappear.

Ashley Madden steered her beat-up Chevy convertible around the final treacherous curve connecting her home-town of Greenwood, South Carolina, to Cherish, South Carolina. Earlier, a storm had kicked up, leaving a debris of tree branches and leaves. Fortunately, the trip took less than two hours to drive by car.

The route led her through the center of the town, which boasted peaceful, immaculate streets, brick-paved sidewalks, and a decided lack of skyscrapers.

She lowered her car window, drew in a breath of a rain-soaked breeze, and snagged the last peanut butter cup from her stash. She took a bite and exhaled a contented sigh.

Unhealthy food was definitely the tastiest.

Her gaze fixed on the road ahead, and she eased up on the gas pedal as she neared her destination. She kept her chin high, her eyes alert. This artist needed to be found, and she intended to find him. She was determined to preserve her free art program for handicapped children and their families low on funds.

Art made people think, made people feel. Art inspired her students to dance and jump up and down with joy.

And art lasted a long time—certainly longer than her relationship with her ex, who'd dumped her with a quick text:

Sorry it didn't work out between us.

And just like that, the relationship was over.

She eased her convertible into the first available parking space near Thumbs Up, a plant retail store and greenhouse. Squinting in the rearview mirror, she patted down her cowlick. Why couldn't it grow in the same direction as the rest of her hair?

It never occurred to her to fuss with her appearance. She didn't consider herself pretty—she was slight, though her feet were too big. People often remarked on her ready smile, though.

Today, she'd dressed in her typical uniform of a plain white T-shirt and chambray shorts. She couldn't imagine styling her honey-blond, shoulder-length hair other than tying it in a haphazard ponytail. Her makeup ritual consisted of sunscreen and a rosy lip gloss.

She shut off the ignition, unbuckled her seatbelt, then walked across the damp grass to the entrance of the greenhouse. Thick summer air hung heavy, the sun appearing through a gauze of humidity.

She shaded her eyes and peered at the sky. God's golden assurance, sunlight, was forever faithful. Regardless of the rain, He repeatedly guaranteed something better was around the corner.

Ashley entered the greenhouse, instantly recognizing the dark-haired woman engrossed in watering a pot of mauve African violets.

"Sarah?" Ashley came up behind her and tapped her on the shoulder.

Sarah whirled. "Ashley! Twinkle!"

Ashley smiled. Her nickname from a precious student. The name had stuck.

Sarah set the watering can to the side and tugged the apron from her slim waist. "How was the drive?"

"The roads are a mess from the windstorm." Ashley spoke slowly to help Sarah read her lips. Sarah had been diagnosed recently with a hearing loss and wore hearing aids.

"Were the roads littered with trees?"

"It could've been worse." Ashley embraced her friend in a hug. "However, I'm here and I'm fine."

"I'm due for my lunch break. Will you help me haul these

bags to the storeroom first?" Sarah pointed to several bags of soil and sheepishly smiled.

Ashley returned the smile. "Of course."

Afterward, they headed toward the rear patio. Sarah grabbed a couple of bottles of water, a turkey sandwich on rye bread, chips, and a chocolate bar.

"Want to share?" She handed Ashley a bottle of water.

"Sure." Ashley slid onto a picnic table beneath a pink-flowered crepe myrtle tree. "I'll take the candy."

Sarah sat across from Ashley and whispered a prayer of grace before unwrapping the sandwich.

Ashley opened her candy bar. Chocolate, her favorite. "Any luck locating David Fodero?" she asked.

Sarah unwrapped her sandwich. "You mean, your reclusive painter?"

"He's not *my* painter. He's Nancy Trainor's painter," Ashley corrected between bites.

Sarah frowned. "Why would an artist like David have his work carried in a small gallery in a tiny southern town?"

"He and Nancy studied together in New York City. She decided her talent lay more in finding and promoting artists than in being an artist." Thoughtfully, Ashley chewed. "David is happy to help out her gallery by having her represent him."

Sarah raised an eyebrow. "Doesn't his artwork sell for tens of thousands of dollars?"

"He allows his works to be sold for lower prices in her gallery. The smaller pieces, not his large canvases." Ashley took another bite of her candy bar. "Without his paintings to sell, her gallery may close. The income his works provide allows her showroom to remain open. Luckily, he's prolific."

"Which implies your art studio will also be shuttered if he disappeared for a long haul," Sarah said.

"No one will rent me space as inexpensively as Nancy

does. Plus, her showroom is a source of inspiration for my kids."

"So David Fodero isn't *your* painter, but the kids in your program are yours?"

Ashley grinned. "Every child is unique, and I love them all for their special talents and gifts."

She'd worked hard to make ends meet to provide for her students—whether it was brushes, soap, or an artist's table—and it was all worth it. Truly, she was blessed. She adored teaching kids and had shaped a satisfying career for herself.

"Maybe you can persuade David to donate funds for your art supplies." Sarah grabbed a chip. "He's certainly wealthy enough."

"If I can ever find him, I just might."

"Poor unsuspecting fellow." Sarah threw Ashley a smirk. "He doesn't realize what he's in for. You don't put the brakes on until you achieve your goals."

"Poor unsuspecting, *mysterious* fellow," Ashley amended.

"It's odd no one has been able to reach him." Again, Sarah offered Ashley half her sandwich. At Ashley's refusal, Sarah happily finished it. "I wonder what happened."

"These genius artists are impossible. Nancy said he's very serious and oftentimes difficult. She walks on eggshells when she deals with him."

"I researched him on the internet." Sarah stood, indicating her break was over. "He is celebrated for his avant-garde portrayal of everyday subjects. Have you seen his *Woman by the River*?"

"That painting has been analyzed and torn apart by critics, though it's a fan favorite. When Nancy displayed it in her showroom, a student of mine, a nine-year-old girl with Down syndrome, continuously stared at it and smiled." Ashley's eyes welled. Her emotions, her affection for each precious child, brimmed inside her. "The girl didn't need any language to convey how she felt."

Sarah gave Ashley's hand a squeeze. "You care too much for people. You're eternally optimistic."

"I can't help it."

"That's why you're special. Don't ever change." Sarah retrieved the discarded wrappers and tossed them in the trash, along with their water bottles. Arm in arm, the women revisited the outside garden center before doubling back inside.

"For the record." Sarah's forehead furrowed. "I never figured out where the river actually was in David's painting."

"Neither did I."

"Who is the woman with the chestnut-brown hair in the corner?"

"Art enthusiasts have speculated about that for years. He's been photographed with every leading actress on the planet. Perhaps the woman is one of them."

Ashley well remembered the day David Fodero had stridden into Nancy's showroom, the one and only time she ever saw him. He'd worn scruffy jeans and a casual navy-blue T-shirt. Yet he looked as handsome as when he'd been photographed wearing a black tuxedo at a glitzy fundraiser. His picture had been splashed on several society pages the following morning.

Nancy had confided he was growing tired of the endless social functions that demanded his attention, and he sought clean air and a calmer lifestyle in Cherish, a small Southern town not far from Greenwood.

Sarah gazed at the ceiling, as if David might miraculously appear. "He's drop-dead gorgeous, and every female on Earth wants to date him."

"Except you."

"I'm happily married to Max. But you're single."

"Yes." Ashley sighed. "Now and forever."

"Never say never." Sarah examined the African violet. Satisfied, she smiled. "Don't lose heart because of one failed relationship."

Don't lose heart.

What woman wouldn't lose heart after being dropped by a guy she'd dated on and off since college? Well-meaning acquaintances speculated she'd set the bar too high. Perhaps her ex couldn't live up to her expectations.

Which were what, exactly?

To show up when he promised her a date at the movies? To phone when he was out of town for long weekends?

Was there a man anywhere who was true to his word, a man who would sincerely care about her, and loved God as much as she did?

She shook off her reflections.

"I'm here on business to help Nancy." Ashley admired a particularly lush plant with cherry-red blossoms and considered buying it. However, she wasn't certain the plant would survive. Unlike her friend, her thumb was the opposite of green. "Nothing more."

"Unfortunate." Sarah sighed dramatically.

"Why?"

"You and David both like art. You couldn't ask for more."

"We're from two different orbits. He lives in New York City with a population of eight and a half million, while Greenwood has, what, five thousand residents?"

"Greenwood and Cherish are similar in size."

"A similarity we don't share with New York City." Ashley couldn't help a giggle. "It'll take more than art appreciation to ignite a spark between David and me. A distinguished painter and a woman who can't draw a stick figure to save her life isn't an ideal match."

"Perhaps." Sarah waggled her eyebrows.

Sarah, the incurable romantic. The women had shared a relaxed candor ever since they'd attended a friend's wedding five years earlier.

Bending, Sarah checked the water level of a particularly dry-looking violet. "David is better looking than your ex."

"Looks aren't everything."

"Looks are something."

"My ex is currently dating a knockout." Uttering the words aloud hurt, and Ashley pressed her lips together. "I saw them together at an upscale restaurant. Luckily, they didn't see me."

"You're a knockout too."

"Thank you." Ashley gnawed her bottom lip. Her ex had stripped away her self-confidence. In fact, he'd been cheating on her the entire time they'd dated. "However, I don't trust men anymore."

"All men?"

"Men in general."

"You enjoy reading romance novels."

"Those men are fictional."

"Never give up. Love will arrive when you least expect it." Sarah's tone was low and steady. "By the way, I discovered why David came to Cherish. Marge Addyson, the pastor of Memorial Street Church, commissioned him to paint a church portrait for their one-hundredth-anniversary cele-bration."

"And?"

"Last week, he was spotted on the church steps taking photos. Tall man with longish black hair, a trimmed beard, and crystal blue eyes, correct?"

"Yes. Or you could just say *brilliant and gorgeous.*"

"Uh, huh. So I've heard."

Ashley belatedly pondered the wisdom of her description, although it was her first thought whenever she pictured him.

Sarah slid her a wise glance. "You know him better than any of the Cherish residents."

"I don't, because we never formally met. I only laid eyes on him for an instant when he appeared in Nancy's showroom to drop off a sketch. I was sitting on the floor of my adjacent studio, stenciling with an eleven-year-old boy. David glanced my way before he chatted with Nancy and gave me his legendary, wry smile."

"What did you do?"

"I smiled back, and we exchanged a friendly wave. His entire conversation with Nancy lasted all of five minutes before he dashed out the door."

She'd estimated he was several inches taller than her, which placed him at over six feet. Muscular and tanned, his physique contrasted sharply with her image of an artist—a thin, whiskered chap sporting a beret and wielding a paintbrush. David's broad shoulders and masculine features were a stark reminder he was light-years beyond her—a teacher who spent her days amidst classes of giggling children, hanging art pieces on austere gray walls while complimenting drawings of princess castles.

Ashley shifted from foot to foot. "Nancy just sold his last oil painting and is adamant about connecting with him."

Much as she wanted to help her friend, Ashley's search for David Fodero was self-serving. Her studio and a café owned by a friend were both connected to Nancy's bustling gallery—a setup that benefitted all three businesses. If any failed, all would be left on rocky financial ground.

Ashley and Sarah reentered the store part of the nursery and were hit with a blast of cold air. The whir of an air conditioner ensured customer comfort from the relentless seasonal heat.

"People say he stays to himself and lives out on the edge of town." Sarah grabbed a metal watering can and filled it with water from a hose. "When my husband went bird-watching at Juniper Mountain yesterday, he saw David standing by his easel near a grove of trees."

"Where is Juniper Mountain?"

Sarah reached in her pocket and pulled out a discarded receipt. Flipping it over, she drew a makeshift map. "The mountain is in the state park. Max hikes the Walnut Forest route."

"Is it difficult?"

"Aren't you an exercise fanatic?"

"Sure. On a treadmill."

"Walnut Forest isn't challenging. David told Max he welcomes the solitude of nature and seemed absorbed in whatever he was painting."

"He is a true artist." Goosebumps rose on Ashley's arms whenever she envisioned his paintings. She speculated about what inspired him to create his pieces—and why he chose certain textures and shades of colors, the scope of the canvases. "I wonder if he finished it."

His landscapes commanded thousands of dollars. It didn't matter what he painted. If patrons discovered his name signed on a canvas, they were willing to pay exorbitant sums.

"Trees, birds, and a pond were in the vicinity. I imagine those were in there somewhere." Sarah set down the watering can and began pruning a flamboyant-fuchsia flowering petunia. "Folks in town say he's polite, but his responses crackle the air like a broad band of heat lightning if someone dares to ask a personal question."

"He's known to be reclusive. Anything else?"

"I imagine Max led a painstaking description of all the birds in the park because he's the resident bird watcher." Sarah grinned. "But we all know how fiercely David guards his privacy, so few will infringe on that—not even talkative Max."

"Which may be why he hasn't answered any of Nancy's phone calls or texts for the past three months."

"He donated an oil landscape to Canine Helpers for their annual fundraiser—the cutest depiction of a dachshund who accompanies him everywhere." Sarah pulled dead leaves off the petunia. "At least, I think it's a dachshund in the painting. The dog's body is sketched in blue, and the ears are purple and red."

"Classic rebellious David." Ashley grinned. "Your information is appreciated."

"One more thing."

Ashley glanced at her watch. Sarah had been due to clock in ten minutes earlier. "I won't keep you any longer."

"No worries. I usually work overtime." Sarah brushed a piece of soil off her dark-green pants. "Max spoke with a park ranger who told him David purchased a dilapidated cabin a few miles outside the state grounds. He's been renovating it these past few months."

"That's where he's living? He bought a—Ashley made quote marks in the air—'dilapidated cabin'? He's not renting?"

"No. The cabin is on ten acres, bordered by state land on all three sides."

"What's the name of the road?"

"Pine Knoll Lane, and it's the only habitable property near the park." A wide smile crossed Sarah's face. "If you touch base with the ranger, he'll provide the general location. Although I warn you, solitude seems paramount to David."

"He's becoming a hermit."

"Right. So don't think you can just appear on his doorstep."

"I'm not here to marry him."

*** End of Excerpt: A Summer to Cherish by Josie Riviera ***

Keep reading on Amazon. FREE on Kindle Unlimited.

ABOUT THE AUTHOR

Josie Riviera is a *USA TODAY* bestselling author of contemporary, inspirational, and historical sweet romances that read like Hallmark movies. She lives in the Charlotte, NC, area with her wonderfully supportive husband. They share their home with an adorable shih tzu, who constantly needs grooming, and live in an old house forever needing renovations.

To receive my Newsletter and your free sweet romance novella ebook as a thank you gift, sign up HERE.

Become a member of my Read and Review VIP Facebook group for exclusive giveaways and ARCs.

josieriviera.com/

ACKNOWLEDGMENTS

An appreciative thank you to my patient husband, Dave, and our three wonderful children.

ALSO BY JOSIE RIVIERA

Seeking Patience

Seeking Catherine (always Free!)

Seeking Fortune

Seeking Charity

Seeking Rachel

The Seeking Series

Oh Danny Boy

I Love You More

A Snowy White Christmas

A Portuguese Christmas

Holiday Hearts Book Bundle Volume One

Holiday Hearts Book Bundle Volume Two

Holiday Hearts Book Bundle Volume Three

Holiday Hearts Book Bundle Volume Four

Holiday Hearts Book Bundle Volume Five

Candleglow and Mistletoe

Maeve (Perfect Match)

A Love Song To Cherish

A Christmas To Cherish

A Valentine To Cherish

A Christmas Puppy To Cherish

A Homecoming To Cherish

A Summer To Cherish

Romance Stories To Cherish

Romance Stories To Cherish Volume Two

Cherished Hearts Six Book Volume

Aloha To Love

Sweet Peppermint Kisses

Valentine Hearts Boxed Set

1-800-CUPID

1-800-CHRISTMAS

1-800-IRELAND

1-800-SUMMER

1-800-NEW YEAR

The 1-800-Series Sweet Contemporary Romance Bundle

Irish Hearts Sweet Romance Bundle

Holly's Gift

A Chocolate-Box Christmas

A Chocolate-Box New Years

A Chocolate-Box Valentine

A Chocolate-Box Summer Breeze

A Chocolate-Box Christmas Wish

A Chocolate-Box Irish Wedding

Chocolate-Box Hearts

Chocolate-Box Hearts Volume Two

Chocolate-Box Double Hearts

Recipes From The Heart

Leading Hearts

New Year Hearts

SENIOR HEARTS

Summer Hearts

Christmas in the Air (1-800-Book)

A Very Christian Christmas

The 1-800-Series Volume Two

Christmas Tails of the Heart

Cocoa's Christmas Love

Pawfect Christmas Hearts

Pink Coral Island

Most books are available in ebook, audiobook, paperback, Large Print paperback and Hardcover.

Many are FREE on Kindle Unlimited!